DEATH of a
GENTLE LADY

The Hamish Macbeth series

DEATH of a GENTLE LADY

A Hamish Macbeth Murder Mystery

M. C. BEATON

ROBINSON
London

Constable & Robinson Ltd
3 The Lanchesters
162 Fulham Palace Road
London W6 9ER
www.constablerobinson.com

First published in the USA 2008 by
Grand Central Publishing
237 Park Avenue, New York, NY 10017

First UK edition published by Constable,
an imprint of Constable & Robinson 2008

This paperback edition published by Robinson,
an imprint of Constable & Robinson 2009

Copyright © 2008, 2009 M.C. Beaton

The right of M.C. Beaton to be identified as the author
of this work has been asserted by her in accordance with
the Copyright, Designs and Patents Act 1988.

All rights reserved. This book is sold subject to the
condition that it shall not, by way of trade or otherwise,
be lent, re-sold, hired out or otherwise circulated in any
form of binding or cover other than that in which it is
published and without a similar condition including this
condition being imposed on the subsequent purchaser.

A copy of the British Library Cataloguing in
Publication data is available from the British Library

ISBN: 978-1-84529-963-7 (pbk)
ISBN: 978-1-84529-648-3 (hbk)

Printed in Great Britain by Clays Ltd, St Ives plc

3 5 7 9 10 8 6 4

To Leslie Caron
With Love

Hamish Macbeth fans share their reviews . . .

'Treat yourself to an adventure in the Highlands; remember your coffee and scones – for you'll want to stay a while!'

'I do believe I am in love with Hamish.'

'M.C. Beaton's stories are absolutely excellent . . . Hamish is a pure delight!'

'A highly entertaining read that will have me hunting out the others in the series.'

'A new Hamish Macbeth novel is always a treat.'

'Once I read the first mystery I was hooked . . . I love her characters.'

Share your own reviews and comments at
www.constablerobinson.com

Chapter One

There is a lady sweet and kind,
Was never face so pleased my mind;
I did but see her passing by,
And yet I love her till I die.
                              – Thomas Ford

The English who settle in the north of Scotland sometimes find they are not welcome. There is something in the Celtic character that delights in historical grudges. But the exception to the norm was certainly Mrs Margaret Gentle. Gentle in name, gentle in nature, said everyone who came across her.

'Now, there's a real lady for you,' they would murmur as she drifted along the waterfront of Lochdubh in the county of Sutherland, bestowing gracious smiles on anyone she met.

Lavender was her favourite colour. And she wore hats! Dainty straws in summer and sensible felt in winter, and always gloves on her small hands.

No one knew her age, but she was considered to be much older than her looks because she had a son in his late forties and a daughter perhaps a year or two younger. She had silvery white hair, blue eyes, and a small round face, carefully made up. Her small mouth was usually curved in the sort of half smile one sees on classical statues.

She had bought an old mock castle outside Braikie. It stood on the edge of the cliffs, a tall square building with two turrets. Mrs Gentle's afternoon tea parties were in great demand. For some reason, she preferred to shop in the village of Lochdubh which only boasted one general store and post office rather than favouring the selection of shops in Braikie.

Perhaps the only person who did not like her was Hamish Macbeth, the local policeman. He said she made his skin crawl, but no one would listen to him. The Currie twins, village spinsters, shook their heads and said that it was high time he married because he had turned against all women.

Mrs Gentle had moved to the Highlands about a year ago. Hamish had waited until she was settled in and then called on her.

As he had approached the castle, he had heard voices coming from the garden at the back and ambled around the side.

His first sight of Mrs Gentle was not a favourable one. She was berating a tall, awkward-looking woman whom he soon learned was her daughter. 'Really, Sarah,' she was saying, her voice shrill, 'it's not my fault that Allan divorced you. I mean, take a look in the mirror. Who'd want you?'

Hamish was about to beat a retreat, but she saw him before he could. Immediately her whole manner went through a lightning change.

She tripped daintily forward to meet him. She was wearing a long lavender skirt and a lavender chiffon blouse. On her head was a little straw hat embellished with silk violets.

'Our local bobby,' she trilled. 'Please come inside. Will you have some tea? Isn't it hot? I didn't think it could get as hot as this in the north of Scotland.'

'I've come at a bad time,' said Hamish.

'Oh, nonsense. Children, you know. They'd break your heart.' Her daughter had disappeared. Mrs Gentle hooked her arm in his and led him into the cool of the old building. Hamish remembered hearing it was a sort of folly built in the nineteenth century by a coalmine owner. It was perilously near the edge of the cliffs, and Hamish shrewdly guessed that she had probably managed to buy it for a very reasonable price.

The drawing room was country-house elegant with graceful antique furniture and paintings in gilt frames on the walls. She urged

3

him to sit down and rang a little silver bell. A tall, blonde, statuesque girl appeared. 'Tea, please,' ordered Mrs Gentle.

'Is that one of your family?' asked Hamish.

Again that trill of laughter. 'My dear man, do I look as if I could have given birth to a Brunhild like that? That's my maid. I think she's from Slovenia or Slovakia or one of those outlandish places. I got her through an agency in Inverness. Now tell me all about yourself.'

Hamish suppressed a frisson of dislike. Perhaps, he thought as he chatted amiably about his police work, it was because of that remark to her daughter he had overheard.

Tea was served; a splendid tea. Hamish felt too uncomfortable to enjoy it. He later described his experience to his friend Angela Brodie, the doctor's wife, as 'drowning in syrup.'

He left as soon as he could. As he stood outside the front door, he noticed that the lace on one of his large regulation boots was untied. He bent down to fix it.

Behind him, inside the house, he heard a voice he recognized as Sarah's. 'Well, have you finished oiling all over the village bobby?'

Then came Mrs Gentle's voice: 'Such a clown, my dear. Improbable red hair and about seven feet tall. These highlanders!'

'If you don't like highlanders, you should

get back down south, Mother. Of course you can't, can you? Can't play lady of the manor down there.'

Hamish walked off slowly. He felt uneasy. He had felt it before when some incomer had started to spread an evil atmosphere around the peace of the Highlands.

'Evil!' exclaimed Angela Brodie when he met her later on a sunny afternoon on the waterfront. 'That's a bit strong. Everyone adores her. Do you know, she has just promised a large sum of money to the church to help with the restoration of the roof?'

'I still don't like her,' grumbled Hamish. His cat, Sonsie, and his dog, Lugs, lay at his feet, panting in the sunshine. 'I should get the animals indoors where it's cool.'

'Have you heard from Elspeth?' Elspeth Grant, once a local reporter, was now working at a Glasgow newspaper: Hamish had toyed too long with the idea of marrying her so she had become engaged to a fellow reporter. But the reporter had jilted her on their wedding day.

'No,' said Hamish curtly.

'Or Priscilla?'

'Neither.'

Hamish moved off. He liked Angela but he wished she would not ferret about in his love life – or lack of it. He had once been engaged to Priscilla Halburton-Smythe, daughter of a colonel who ran the local hotel, but had ended the engagement because of her chilly nature.

In the comparative coolness of the police station, where he also lived, he suddenly felt he was being overimaginative. Mrs Gentle was, in his opinion, a pretentious bitch. But to think of her as evil was going too far.

Autumn arrived early, bringing gusty gales and showers of rain sweeping in from the Atlantic to churn up the waters of the sea loch at Lochdubh. Hamish was involved in coping with a series of petty crimes. His beat was large because the police station in the nearby village of Cnothan had been closed down. He was soon to find out that his own station had come up again on the list of closures. The news came from Detective Inspector Jimmy Anderson, who called one blustery Saturday.

'Got any whisky?' he asked, sitting at the kitchen table and shrugging off his coat.

'You're not getting any,' said Hamish. 'Have coffee. You'll get caught one day and off the force you'll go.'

'You'll want a dram yourself when you hear what I have to say,' said Jimmy.

'What's that?'

'You'd best start selling off your livestock.'

Hamish kept sheep and hens. 'This police station is being put up for sale.'

Hamish sank into a chair opposite Jimmy, his hazel eyes troubled. 'Tell me about it.'

'Do you ken a woman called Gentle?'

'Oh, her, aye. What's she got to do with it?'

'It's like this. I was at a Rotary dinner last night –'

'I didn't know you were a member of the Rotary Club.'

'Not me. But Sergeant MacAllister couldn't go and gave me his ticket. Anyway, the super was there, and Blair.'

Detective Chief Inspector Blair was the bane of Hamish's life.

'And? What's this Gentle female got to do with it?'

'Well, she was seated between Superintendent Daviot and Blair. They were all over her. She was fluttering and flirting – odd at her age.'

'Get to the point, man.'

'I went to have a pee and when I got back into the room, I heard her say your name. My place was at the other end o' the table, but I waited for a bit. She was saying that she was surprised that the police would go to the cost of maintaining a police station in Lochdubh when everyone knew you did practically nothing.

'Daviot said you were a good officer and had solved a lot of murders. Blair weighed in and said there weren't any murders now and

7

no drug problems because most of the young people went south to the cities. He said that house prices were astronomical these days and that the police could get a lot of money for your station. Mrs Gentle shook her little head and said sadly that you were short on social skills – that you had called on her without an invitation and stayed eating her out of house and home before she could get rid of you.

'Then Blair turned round and saw me and demanded to know what I thought I was doing, so I didn't hear any more.'

'That woman iss a slimy wee bitch!' raged Hamish, his accent becoming more sibilant as it always did when he was angry.

'Well, maybe. But she charmed the socks off all the bigwigs.'

The phone in the police office rang. Hamish went to answer it. It was Daviot's secretary, Helen, telling him to report to headquarters at the earliest opportunity.

Hamish trailed back into the kitchen. 'I've been summoned.'

Superintendent Daviot smoothed back the silver wings of his carefully barbered hair and tugged at the lapels of his expensively tailored suit before instructing his secretary to send Hamish in.

'Sit down, Hamish,' he said. 'Helen, some tea and biscuits would be nice.'

Hamish noticed the triumphant gleam in Helen's eyes, and his heart sank. Helen detested him.

'Now, er, Hamish,' said Daviot. 'It has come to my attention that there is not enough work up there for a man of your skills. We have a big drug problem here in Strathbane, and we need good officers. Ah, thank you, Helen. No, we will serve ourselves.'

When the door closed behind the secretary, he went on. 'A man like you should be taking the detective exams with a view to joining the CID.'

'May I say something, sir?'

'By all means. Have an Abernethy biscuit or would you like a Penguin?'

'Tea will be fine. Mrs Gentle is a vicious woman. Do not listen to a word she says.'

'I use my own judgement, Macbeth,' said the super, colouring up. 'But since you have raised the lady's name, it seems you imposed on her hospitality.'

'I called on her as part of my duties. As you know, I frequently call on people on my beat. She was having a spiteful row with her daughter. She likes to create the image of being perfect. I was not to be forgiven for having witnessed her at her worst. Such is the way of psychopaths like her.'

9

'Macbeth! I have met the lady and consider myself to be a good judge of character. She is charming and kind, very much a lady. You don't see many of them like her these days.'

'No, thank God.'

Daviot's face hardened. 'That's enough. You have six months. You will be supplied with a flat in police accommodation in Strathbane. And no pets. You'll need to get rid of that odd cat of yours, and the dog. You may go.'

Hamish stood up. 'You should keep me where I am, sir, because there's going to be a murder.'

'What murder?'

'Mrs Gentle.'

'Get off with you!'

Jimmy waylaid Hamish on the way out.

'Well?'

'That Gentle woman's done the damage all right. I'm losing the station, I'm to move into one o' thae poxy police flats, and no pets. I'm going to resign. Mind you, I went over the top and called Mrs Gentle a psychopath and said someone was going to murder her.'

'Come and have a drink. One for the road.'

'All right.'

As soon as they were in the bar and seated over their drinks, Jimmy lit a cigarette. 'That's against the law,' exclaimed Hamish. 'No smoking in Scotland.'

'So sue me. Do you care?'

'Someone might report you.'

'Like who? Nothing but coppers in here, and the barman smokes himself.'

'Be a good lad and put it out. I'm not going to sit here, aiding and abetting a crime.'

'Oh, all right, Mother. Are you just going to take this lying down? Last time the villagers got up a petition.'

'I'm weary. I seem to have been living under constant threat of eviction for years. But I tell you one thing, before I leave, I'm going to get that woman out of the Highlands.'

'How?'

'Wait and see.'

Back in Lochdubh, Hamish began to gossip busily. The news of his forthcoming eviction and subsequent loss of his pets spread like wildfire throughout Sutherland. Matthew Campbell, the local reporter, wrote up the story, saying that Hamish's banishment had been instigated at a Rotary dinner by Mrs Gentle, a newcomer to the Highlands.

Mrs Gentle, arriving back in Lochdubh a week later followed by her tall maid, felt a definite chill in the air that had nothing to do with the clear autumn day. It was as if she suddenly did not exist. People avoided eye contact. Her greetings went unnoticed. Mr Patel, who ran the local store, packed up her groceries in silence.

Her temper was rising, but she masked it well. As she left the shop, she met Mrs Wellington, the minister's wife. At that moment, Mrs Wellington was more interested in the repairs to the church roof than the banishment of Hamish Macbeth.

'Good morning,' she said breezily. 'A fine brisk day. I hate to rush you but my husband needs that cheque for the repairs to the church roof.'

Mrs Gentle gave her little curved smile. 'What cheque?'

'You promised to donate a generous amount of money towards the church.'

'Did I? How stupid of me. I am holding a family reunion next week and I have just discovered I am quite low in funds. Such a pity. I am sure you will find the money somehow.'

Mrs Gentle returned home in a bad mood. The sight of her daughter slumped in front of the television set with a large gin and tonic in her hand made her erupt into rage. She switched off the set, walked round, and stared down at her daughter.

12

'Sarah, I want you out of here after the family get-together.'

'But you asked me up here. You said I could stay as long as I liked.'

'I've changed my mind. I'm changing my will as well. It's time you got a job.'

'But I'm fifty, Mother.'

'You'll find something. Andrew has a good job.' Her son, Andrew, was a stockbroker. 'The grandchildren are doing well. You've always been a failure. Ayesha, take that stuff into the kitchen and stop gaping.' The maid went off. Mrs Gentle watched her go, then followed her into the kitchen. Ayesha had been working as a maid in a London hotel when Mrs Gentle had offered her the job although she maintained the fiction that she had hired the girl through an agency.

'I never asked you what country you came from,' said Mrs Gentle.

'Turkey,' said Ayesha, putting groceries away. 'Izmir.'

That curved smile again. 'Dear me, I thought all Turks were dark.'

'Not all,' said Ayesha. 'Some of us are quite fair.'

'Let me see, Turkey is not in the European Union. I do hope you have a work permit. Silly me. I never asked you.'

Ayesha flushed to the roots of her hair. 'I was studying at London University, but my

13

student visa ran out. I needed money, so I worked in a hotel.'

'I can't have an illegal alien working for me. Wait until after the family party and then you must leave or I will have to report you to the police.'

'Oh, please. Can't you apply to the Home Office for me?'

'Don't be silly. Oh, don't start to cry. Get on with your work.'

Hamish Macbeth was just settling down to a dinner of comfort food – haggis, mashed potatoes, and mashed turnips – when he heard the front doorbell ring. The locals never used the front door, which had jammed with the damp ages ago. He went to the door and shouted through the letter box, 'Come round to the side door.'

He went and opened the kitchen door. Round the side of the police station came a tall figure he recognized as Mrs Gentle's maid.

When he ushered her into the kitchen, he noticed her eyes were red with crying.

'Sit down,' he said. 'What's the matter, lassie?'

'I have come to be arrested.'

'I'm just about to eat, and there's enough for two,' said Hamish.

'I can't eat.'

'Oh, you'll feel better.' He got another plate and put a generous helping on it for her. 'Now eat and tell me about it.'

Ayesha picked at her food as she told him that she was in the country illegally and had lost her job.

'I can't be bothered arresting anyone at the moment,' said Hamish.

She really was very beautiful, he thought. She was nearly as tall as he was himself, with a splendid figure in hip-hugging jeans, a T-shirt, and a denim jacket. Her hair looked a natural gold, she had high cheekbones and a perfect mouth.

'What is your name?' he asked.

'Ayesha Tahir. Turkish.'

'I didn't know there were blonde Turks.'

'Some are.' She took a mouthful of food. 'This is nice. You are not like a policeman.'

'I'm not going to be one much longer, thanks to Mrs Gentle putting the poison in.'

'The poison?'

'She managed to persuade my bosses that my services were not needed in Lochdubh.'

'Can't you stop her?'

'I can't stop anything now. I'm going to resign.'

Hamish clasped his hands behind his head and stared at the ceiling. 'Why should I arrest you?' he asked.

'Like I said, Mrs Gentle has found out that

my visa has expired. She says I can stay until after her family party and then I've got to leave.'

'Have you got your passport with you?'

'Yes, in my bag.' She fished it out and handed it to him.

Hamish flicked through the passport, studied the visa, and then said, 'Would you like to leave this with me? I might be able to do something.'

Hope shone in her blue eyes. 'Do you think it possible?'

'Maybe. But you're not to talk to anyone at all about it. I see you're twenty-five years old. That's not young for a student.'

'My father wanted me to marry a local businessman. I stalled. I said I would if I could get an education first. I studied English at Istanbul University. When I got my degree, I applied for permit to further my studies at London University and received three years to gain a PhD. When I got my degree, I applied for a work permit but was refused. I started to work as a maid in a hotel. It was the only work I could get. Then Mrs Gentle stayed at the hotel. I was cleaning her room. She offered me work. She seemed so kind. It was a great mistake.'

'Finish your meal and come back here as soon as the family party is over. I might have something for you then.'

* * *

16

Peter Brimley, a small wizened man, opened his door in a side street of Inverness the following day and scowled up at the tall figure of Hamish Macbeth.

'Whit now?' he snarled. 'I've done my time and I'm going straight.'

'I'd like to come in. I'm here to offer you money for some of your skills.'

'This is a frame-up?'

'Don't be daft. I won't want to get found out even more than you would. Let me in.'

Hamish walked into Peter's small living room. There was a large desk by the window with a powerful lamp over it. Peter rushed forward and swept a pile of papers into a drawer.

'Going straight, my arse,' said Hamish cheerfully. 'But I am about to join the world of criminals. I want you to forge a passport for me. Well, not forge a passport, chust a visa.'

Peter stared at the floor in mulish silence.

'Come on, man,' said Hamish. 'It's a simple job for a genius like you. I didn't put you away. Inverness police did that.'

Peter shrugged in resignation. 'Let me see the passport.'

Hamish handed it over. Peter went to his desk and sat down. Hamish waited impatiently. At last, he demanded, 'Well?'

'Aye. I could alter it to give her another three years. But that's all.'

'Grand. How soon?'

'Gie me a week. Right. Now to the money.'

Hamish blinked at the price but was in no mood for haggling. 'You'll get your money when I get the altered visa. I'll be back next week.'

Outside, Hamish phoned Ayesha, who had given him her mobile phone number. He told her he might have something for her in a week's time but cautioned her not to breathe a word to anyone. 'Hasn't your father been trying to track you down?' he asked.

'I phoned him two years ago and told him I wasn't coming back. He said I was no daughter of his and he did not want to see me ever again.'

'That's sad, but it makes things less complicated.'

Hamish felt like Santa Claus a week later when he handed Ayesha her altered passport. 'This is wonderful,' she said. 'At least I have three more years.'

Then Hamish had a really mad idea. 'There is something else we could do,' he said.

'What is that, my dear friend?'

'We could get married.'

'What?'

'That way you would become a British citizen, have a British passport, and get work in a school or a university. Then we get a divorce.'

A cynical, wary look entered her blue eyes. 'And what would you get?'

'The fact that I was a married man would make them at headquarters leave me alone for a bit. I happen to know that there are no quarters for married men in Strathbane. I get my police station and you get your passport.'

'What about sex?'

'You know, I've been thinking about that,' said Hamish with almost childish candour. 'You are gorgeous and yet I don't fancy you. No vibes.'

'You will be shocked.'

'I'm a policeman. I'm past being shocked.'

'I am a lesbian.'

'What a waste! I mean, everyone to their own bag. But since we'd be getting married just for appearances, it doesn't matter.'

A week later, Elspeth Grant was sitting at the reporters' desk at the *Daily Bugle* newspaper office in Glasgow dreaming of the Highlands. She thought it was high time she went back for a holiday. She wondered how Hamish was getting on and if he ever thought of her.

A colleague came up to her and said, 'I've got the job of trawling through the local Scottish papers for stories to follow up. Didn't you know that policeman in Lochdubh, Hamish Macbeth?'

'What's happened to him?' asked Elspeth anxiously.

'He's getting married, that's what, and to some girl with a foreign name.'

'Let me see.'

There it was in black and white in the *Highland Times*, an announcement that the marriage of Hamish Macbeth to Ayesha Tahir would take place in the registry office in Inverness on Wednesday, in two weeks' time.

Elspeth felt miserable. Hamish hadn't married her, but the consolation was always that he hadn't married anyone else.

Colonel Halburton-Smythe phoned his daughter Priscilla, who was working in London. 'Hamish Macbeth is getting married in a couple of weeks, and to some foreigner.'

Priscilla held the receiver so tightly that her knuckles stood out white. 'Who is this female?'

'Some Turk who was working as a maid for one of the locals. Stunning-looking girl.'

He went on to talk about the running of the hotel while Priscilla barely listened. Hamish! To be married!

Chapter Two

Marriage is a desperate thing.
— John Selden

Hamish Macbeth was thoroughly miserable. After all the red tape had been gone through and he had permission to marry Ayesha and had returned triumphantly to tell her the news, it was to find that Mrs Gentle had taken over.

He raged at Ayesha, who had just informed him that Mrs Gentle had not only promised Ayesha a generous gift of money and said the reception should be held in her home, but even paid up for the church roof. She was restored in the eyes of the highlanders to local saint.

Hamish, hearing all this horrible news from Ayesha at the police station, said grimly, 'Then the wedding is off.'

Ayesha looked at him with cold eyes. 'If you cancel this wedding, I will tell everyone you got my visa forged.'

'Then you'd be deported.'

'If you don't marry me, I'll be deported anyway.'

Hamish, normally easy-going, could feel himself in the grip of a blind rage. The news of his forthcoming marriage had made his bosses relent and promise that he could keep his police station. If he cancelled it, his station would be under threat again.

Mrs Gentle was sitting over her accounts, scowling at them. She was regretting her generosity. She had guessed Hamish Macbeth was behind her recent fall from grace and, knowing that he would be furious with her for taking over the wedding arrangements, had done just that. She had supplied Ayesha with a wedding outfit. But now she had learned that a highland wedding reception was a free-for-all. Everyone from around the Highlands, from gamekeepers to fishermen and forestry workers, would be cramming into her elegant home. She tapped her pen against her still-perfect teeth. Then there was that ridiculous sum of money she had promised Ayesha. Something about the girl had made her uneasy. What had she overheard when the family had been in the castle for that reunion?

She rang the little silver bell on her desk. When Ayesha appeared, Mrs Gentle said with her sweetest smile, 'I am doing a lot for you.'

'And I am so grateful,' said Ayesha.

'The fact is, it is all more than I can really afford. I am afraid I won't be able to give you the ten thousand pounds I promised you.'

'I need that money!' exclaimed Ayesha.

'My dear girl, you are to be married.'

'A policeman does not earn much.'

'Then get a job!'

Ayesha looked down at her and said in carefully measured tones, 'If you do not give me the money, I will tell everyone about you. I will tell them everything I overheard at that family party of yours.'

Mrs Gentle turned in her chair and looked up at her. For one moment, Ayesha felt frightened. Mrs Gentle's eyes were full of hate and venom. But then she turned away and said quietly, 'I'll see what I can do, Ayesha.'

Hamish Macbeth's wedding day. Only a few villagers were going to attend the ceremony in Inverness: the rest would congregate at Mrs Gentle's for the reception.

Jimmy Anderson was to act as best man. Ayesha had arrived the evening before and left two large suitcases at the police station. Hamish realized he would need to let her have his bedroom while he slept in the cell. His dog, Lugs, and his wild cat, Sonsie, had sensed their master's misery. Whenever Ayesha appeared, Lugs growled and Sonsie glared at the girl with baleful eyes.

Jimmy found Hamish sitting at his kitchen table in his dressing gown. 'Come on, man,' he cried. 'Get a move on.'

Hamish sighed and uncoiled himself from his chair. 'What's up, laddie?' asked Jimmy. 'You're going to marry the most smashing-looking girl.'

'Wedding nerves,' said Hamish bleakly.

Urged on by Jimmy, he dressed quickly in his best suit. Jimmy was to drive him to Inverness.

'The super's going to be there,' said Jimmy. 'He's organized a guard of coppers, crossed truncheons when you leave as a married man.'

Hamish grunted by way of reply. He thought a large noose hanging outside the registry office would be more appropriate. How could he have been such a fool? He admitted to himself that he had done it not only to keep his beloved police station and his cat and dog, but out of his malicious highland streak which wanted to imagine what Priscilla and Elspeth would both think when they heard the news.

His mother and father were delighted. He could hardly let them know of the mistake he had made. They were travelling to Inverness from Rogart for the ceremony and had forgiven him for not having introduced them to his fiancée.

When Hamish arrived at the registry office, he was only dimly aware of a sea of faces. Then he saw his mother looking at him with anxious eyes and went and hugged her.

The horrible Mrs Gentle had promised to be Ayesha's bridesmaid. Hamish went into the entrance hall of the registry and waited for his bride-to-be with hatred in his heart.

And waited.

Superintendent Daviot approached. 'Time's getting on, Hamish, and the registrar has another wedding to perform this morning.'

'I'll phone her and see what's keeping her.' Hamish dialled Ayesha's mobile. It rang and rang and then switched over to the answering service.

'No good,' he said.

'Phone Mrs Gentle,' said Jimmy. 'She's supposed to be bringing her.'

'I don't have her number.'

'I'll get it from directory enquiries,' said Jimmy. He moved off.

After five minutes, he came back. 'I'm right sorry, Hamish. Mrs Gentle says she can't find her. She said she went out for a walk very early and never came back.'

Blair's face loomed up, a fat grin on it. 'She's stood you up,' he said.

Somewhere inside Hamish was the beginning of a little warm glow of relief.

* * *

Mrs Gentle's home was crammed with villagers. She had tried to turn them away, but they had retaliated by saying it was a shame to let good food and drink go to waste and simply walked in. Not only that, but they had found the wedding presents laid out for display in the morning room and begun to take them back.

A band had turned up and had begun to play, and the house echoed to the sound of accordion, fiddle, and drums.

Hamish returned to the police station after having assured his family that he would be all right. There was an hysterical message on the answering machine from Mrs Gentle, demanding that he come to her house immediately and tell everyone to go home. He had told Jimmy to go to the reception, adding that he would be along as soon as he could.

When Jimmy had left, he went into the bedroom and flung the first of Ayesha's suitcases on to the bed. It was not locked. He opened it and rummaged around. Then he opened the other one. In the flap at the back of the suitcase, he found a wallet. It contained ten thousand pounds in crisp notes and Ayesha's passport. He put the money back in the wallet and took the passport with him into the kitchen. He took the lid off his unlit wood-

26

burning stove and dropped it in. It could stay there, he thought grimly, until he found out where she had gone. Then he set out for the castle.

He was not surprised to find that Jimmy had joined the revellers and was standing, grinning, and holding a large glass of whisky. There was a silence as Hamish walked in.

'Please leave,' he said. 'This is a sad day for me, and you should not be celebrating.'

They slowly left, clutching wedding presents.

When the last one had gone, including Jimmy, Hamish said to Mrs Gentle, 'We need to have a talk before I contact police headquarters.'

'What about?' Mrs Gentle's usually dulcet tones were now harsh. 'She's run away rather than marry you. Accept it.'

'It's not as easy as that,' said Hamish heavily. 'I had a quick look through the suitcases she left with me. I found a wallet with ten thousand pounds in it.'

'Oh, goody. That's mine and I want it back. I gave it to her as a wedding present.'

'Very generous.'

'I have been too damn generous. Look at my home! Food trodden into the carpets.'

'I do not think she would have run away and left all her things, along with the money,' said Hamish. 'I am afraid I will need to keep your money until the enquiry is over.'

27

'What enquiry?' she screeched. 'You stupid man. She ran away from you, that's all.'

'When did you last see her?'

'This morning, early. She said she wanted to go for a walk before changing her clothes and leaving for Inverness. She never returned.'

'Did your daughter see her?'

'Sarah has gone off to London. I am here alone.'

There was a ring at the doorbell. 'I'd better get rid of whoever that is,' said Mrs Gentle. 'Probably one of those villagers come to take their wedding present back. I've never seen such a load of rubbish. Six crystal butter dishes!'

She went out into the hall to answer the door. When she returned, she was followed by Superintendent Daviot and Detective Chief Inspector Blair.

'Hamish,' said Daviot, 'this is a sorry business. It's hardly a police matter, but if you like, we'll check the ports and airports for you.'

'I'm afraid it is a police matter,' said Hamish. 'She's left all her belongings at the police station along with ten thousand pounds, given to her by Mrs Gentle.'

'And her passport?'

'I'll have another look. But I couldn't find it,' lied Hamish. He was worried that if that visa was subjected to police scrutiny, the forgery might be discovered and Peter might be questioned.

'Where is she from?' asked Daviot.

'She said she was from Izmir in Turkey, and that her father wanted her to marry a local businessman so she ran away. The family name is Tahir.'

'Do you have a photograph of her?'

'I do.' Hamish took out his wallet and extracted a photograph. He had taken it outside the police station before he had tried to tell Ayesha that the wedding was off. It showed a laughing Ayesha, tall and beautiful.

'We'll get this wired over to the police in Izmir. I'm very sorry for you, Hamish,' said Daviot. 'Come along now. We'd best leave Mrs Gentle in peace.'

Back at the police station, Hamish found Angela Brodie, local author as well as doctor's wife, waiting for him with his pets. She had promised to look after them while he was in Inverness and then to shut them up in the police station while she went to the reception. But word of the cancelled wedding had spread like fire in the heather, and so she had decided to keep the animals with her until he might return.

'Gamekeeper Jamie phoned me and said he had seen your car heading towards Lochdubh, so here I am to see if I can say or do anything to help you.'

'Nothing at all, Angela. Come ben and have a drink with me.'

After he poured whisky for himself and Angela, he said, 'It's odd. For some reason, Mrs Gentle gave her a present of ten thousand pounds, and yet not so long ago Mrs Gentle had told the girl she was fired. She's left the money in one of her suitcases along with her clothes.'

'May I have a look? Maybe in your distress you missed something.'

'Go ahead. Her cases are in the bedroom.'

He sipped his whisky, calling himself all kinds of fool, aware the whole time of that passport lurking at the bottom of the stove.

Angela came back in. 'It's very odd, Hamish. Didn't you notice her clothes?'

'Not particularly.'

'They are very, very expensive. For example, there are a couple of Versace dresses and an Armani jacket.'

'Maybe her family are wealthy. I've a bad feeling about this. Why didn't she take her clothes? Why did Mrs Gentle who wanted to fire her suddenly decide to give her a wedding reception and pay her ten thousand pounds?'

'I don't believe she's gone,' said Angela. 'No woman would leave behind clothes like that, not to mention ten thousand pounds. She'll turn up.'

'I hope to God I never see her again,' said Hamish bitterly.

'Poor Hamish, you have no luck with women. It's cold in here. I'll light the stove for you.'

'No!' yelled Hamish.

Angela, who had half risen to her feet, looked at him in surprise. 'I'm sorry,' said Hamish quickly. 'It's been a bad day.'

'I'll leave you. Don't get plastered. You'll only wake up in the morning with a hangover.'

Hamish awoke the next morning with a feeling of bleak emptiness. Never before in his life had he felt such a fool. If there was anything sinister about the disappearance of Ayesha, then he had compromised the investigation by lying about her and hiding that passport. But if the police ever got their hands on that passport and sent it away from the incompetent forensic department at Strathbane to Glasgow, say, some eagle-eyed boffin might recognize Peter's handiwork. He had been allowed two weeks' holiday for his honeymoon. Because of Ayesha turning out to be such a blackmailer, he had cancelled any idea of it.

Blackmailer!

Had the girl found out something about Mrs Gentle and been blackmailing her?

Hamish decided to get out of Lochdubh for the day, away from sympathetic callers. He loaded up the Land Rover with his fishing tackle along with his dog and cat and set off for the River Anstey. He didn't have a fishing permit but knew that the water bailiff was lazy; he was sure he wouldn't be discovered.

He returned in the evening with eight trout to find Jimmy Anderson pacing up and down outside the police station.

'Where have you been?' howled Jimmy.'

In the kitchen, Jimmy explained what had happened. Mr Tahir had been located in Turkey, and yes, he had a daughter called Ayesha. But his Ayesha was married and living right there in Izmir. And she *wasn't* the girl in the photo that had been wired to him. Mr Tahir had shown the real Ayesha this picture, and she had recognized the woman.

This was her story. A few years before, the Tahir family had been dining at Istanbul's Pera Palace Hotel. Ayesha had completed her studies at Istanbul and had just received her visa to go to London for her PhD. She had been celebrating with her family. At the next table was a party of thuggish-looking Russians, along with the girl from Hamish's

32

photograph. The Tahirs had been sure that these Russians were mafia, and they were sorry for the girl who, said Ayesha, was being treated like dirt. They thought she was a Natasha, the slang name for a Russian or Eastern European prostitute.

When the Tahirs returned to Izmir, Ayesha realized that her passport was not in her handbag. She thought it must have fallen out somewhere, but while applying for a new one and facing up to all the formalities of getting the visa again, she had fallen in love with a local man and decided to get married instead of furthering her education. So she put the passport right out of her mind.

The police now believed that the fake Ayesha had stolen the passport and run away from whoever was keeping her. Because of the Tahirs' conviction that the men with her back then had looked like Russian mafia and had been talking in Russian, and because she had now left her clothes behind, it looked as if she might have been snatched – or murdered. Her photograph would appear in the local Turkish papers. Istanbul police had a copy and were checking at the Pera Palace Hotel to see if anyone knew anything about the missing girl.

'I think she was blackmailing Mrs Gentle,' said Hamish.

'Why?'

'Mrs Gentle gave her ten thousand pounds cash as a wedding present, she said. Now, one minute Ayesha's sitting here weeping and telling me that Mrs Gentle has given her notice, and the next minute she's telling me that Mrs Gentle is not only giving her money but hosting the reception.'

'Her passport?' asked Jimmy. 'Did you find it?'

Hamish rose and took a bottle of whisky down from a cupboard. With his back to Jimmy, he said, 'No.'

'You know,' said Jimmy, 'I wouldnae mind a black coffee with my whisky.'

'The electric kettle's broken,' said Hamish.

'You never used it. Light the stove. It's cold in here.'

Hamish blushed. 'Can't. The chimney's blocked. The sweep's coming the morrow. Help yourself to whisky. I'll chust put some o' these trout out in the freezer. You'll stay for dinner?'

'No, I'd best be getting back.'

Hamish went out to the shed where he kept the chest freezer. As soon as he had gone, Jimmy took the cleat and lifted the lid of the stove. He felt inside. His hand touched something. He lifted it out. Ayesha's passport. 'Oh, Hamish,' he muttered. 'What have you done?'

Hamish came back and stiffened when he saw the passport lying on the table.

34

'Sit down, laddie,' said Jimmy grimly, 'and spit it out. No lies this time.'

Suddenly weary and ashamed, Hamish sat down at the table and began to tell his story, leaving nothing out.

'You see,' he said finally, 'they'll examine that visa and check with the authorities. They'll realize it's a forgery and start looking around for highland forgers. They'll get to Peter, and he'll sing like a canary to shorten his prison sentence. Not only will my police station go, but my job as well.'

'But why, Hamish? Why did you do it?'

'It was a quixotic gesture. She was so beautiful that all I could think about besides saving my home and animals was letting folk know I wasn't a failure in love. What a mess. I suppose you'd better do your duty.'

Jimmy took a gulp of whisky.

Then he rose and took the passport. He lifted the lid of the stove and dropped it in. He picked up a packet of firelighters, extracted one, ignited it with his lighter, and dropped it in on top of the passport.

'Now we're partners in crime.'

'Thanks, Jimmy. I don't know how . . .'

'Forget it. Let's suppose she had something on Ma Gentle. So Gentle kills the girl. What does she do with the body? Ayesha, or whoever she is, is a great big girl. Mrs Gentle is a wee old woman. Say she hit her hard. With the reception and the house full of people, it would need to be down in the cellar or in one of the upper rooms. Look, I'm off-duty tomorrow. Put me up for the night and we'll go over, all innocent like, and ask if we can see her room. Mrs Gentle can hardly refuse. If she follows us around and looks nervous, say, we might get an idea she's guilty of something.'

Mrs Gentle opened the door to them the next morning, looking flustered. 'What is it? You can't come in. I've got some women from Braikie clearing up the mess.'

'We've found out that Ayesha had stolen someone's identity,' said Jimmy. 'We would just like to look in her room to see if we can find any clues to who she really is.'

'Oh, very well. Follow me.' The sounds of energetic cleaning met their ears. 'I'll be glad when the house is clean again. I spent all day yesterday recruiting women to do the job.' Mrs Gentle walked up the stairs ahead of them, her back erect. A faint smell of lavender perfume drifted back to them.

Mrs Gentle pushed open a door at the top of the house. 'This was her room,' she said.

'*Was*?' repeated Hamish. 'Do you think she's dead?'

'Of course not. If you remember, she was to leave here for good on the day of her wedding.'

Hamish and Jimmy walked in. Jimmy turned round to where Mrs Gentle was hovering in the doorway. 'You can leave us,' he said.

She hesitated a moment and then went slowly away down the stairs.

It was a turret room. Very little furniture. A narrow bed stood against one wall, an old-fashioned wardrobe against another. There was a round table at the window with three hard-backed chairs; on the table was a small television set. No books, no pictures, and no framed photographs.

Hamish opened the wardrobe. There was only one garment, a black fur coat. 'Jimmy, is this mink, would ye say?'

Jimmy felt the fur. 'Aye, it is that. Imagine leaving that . . . maybe she was frightened of animal rights people.'

'We don't get them up here,' said Hamish. There were three drawers at the foot of the wardrobe. He knelt down and opened them. In one he found three sweaters and in another silk underwear, not of the sexy type but knitted silk, the kind used by sportsmen and women when they were out shooting on the moors. The bottom drawer was empty. 'It probably got cold up here,' he said. 'I noticed that there isn't any central heating. She's got money, our Mrs Gentle, but it'd take an awful lot to get central heating into this folly. The fireplace is blocked up.

'I tell you, Jimmy, it's weird. There's nothing personal either here or in her suitcases. I mean, no letters, no jewellery, no photographs.'

'If she turns out to be some sort of Russian tart,' said Jimmy, 'it stands to reason she wouldnae have anything like that.'

'But even tarts have friends, family, someone,' said Hamish. A buffet of wind rattled the windowpanes. He crossed to the window and looked down. 'It must have been like an icebox up here last winter,' he said. 'Why did she stay? Why wasn't she down in one of the cities looking for a rich protector?'

'Probably because of that stolen passport,' said Jimmy. 'And if she was a dolly for the Russian mafia, she might have been scared of a dose of radiation in her tea.'

'I shouldnae think they'd bother,' said Hamish moodily. 'Whoever her protector was, he'd just move on to the next good-looking girl. Now, if anyone wanted to get rid of a body around this castle, where would they dump it?'

'Easy. Over the cliff she goes.'

'I was afraid you'd say that. I'd best get back and pick up my climbing gear.'

As they drove back, Jimmy said, 'You shouldnae be hoping to find a body, my friend.'

'Why?'

'I don't know what's happened to your wits these days. You'd be first suspect.'

'Not me. I was with you and then at the registry office in Inverness.'

'Aye, but if the procurator fiscal got evidence that she'd been killed during the night, where would that leave you?'

'Maybe Mrs Gentle got rid of her. There's something not right about that woman.'

'Havers! That wee woman?'

'Do you know, I ran her name through the police computer. Nothing. I wonder what her maiden name is.'

'Can you see an elderly lady taking on a big strapping Russian lassie? And then getting the body out of the castle and over the cliffs?'

'Look at it this way. Maybe our Russian went out for a walk and was standing on the cliffs. What with the noise of the sea and the wind, she wouldn't hear anyone creeping up behind her. One good shove and down she goes.'

Later when Hamish was stowing his climbing gear in the Land Rover along with his dog and cat, Jimmy complained, 'Do you need to take thae beasties with ye? That wild cat of yours fair gives me the creeps.'

'She's harmless,' said Hamish. Sonsie had been found injured up on the moors, and

Hamish had adopted the animal. Despite dire predictions that a wild cat could not be domesticated, she had settled in and, even stranger, formed a bond with Hamish's dog.

Jimmy sat on the top of the cliffs as Hamish began his slow descent. He looked over once and then shrank back. He pulled a flask out of his pocket and took a swig of whisky. Seagulls sailed overhead, screeching and diving. A few puffins, like fussy little men in tailcoats, came out of their burrows and stared at him.

At last, Hamish came back. 'It's high tide,' he said. 'I'll wait for low tide and go back down.'

'And when's low tide?'

'Two hours' time.'

'I hope you don't except me to sit here on this draughty hilltop for four hours.'

'We'll go into Braikie and get something to eat.'

In Braikie, Jimmy looked around The Highlanders Arms in amazement. 'It's the spirit o' John Knox,' he said. 'If you're going to drink, you are not going to enjoy yourself. I didnae know places like this still existed.'

It was a dimly lit establishment with tables scarred with old cigarette burns. The floor was covered in dark green greasy linoleum. The bar and the shelves behind looked as if they had not been cleaned in a long time.

'Eat your pie and peas.'

'I might get salmonella.'

'The pies come from the bakery. They're all right.'

'I still don't know how you let yourself nearly get trapped into marriage,' said Jimmy.

'I told you,' said Hamish huffily. 'I thought I was going to have to leave the force in order to keep my dog and cat. I thought I was doing a grand thing. Anyway, she told me she was a lesbian.'

'That figures. A lot of tarts are. She could hae been lying, of course. Didn't fancy you.'

'Oh, shut up.'

When they arrived back at the clifftop, Jimmy elected to stay in the Land Rover. The rising wind buffeted the car. His eyes began to droop, and soon he was fast asleep.

He awoke with a start. Hamish had wrenched open the door. 'I've got to phone air-sea rescue,' he shouted. 'Body at the foot of the cliffs.'

'Is it her?'

'No. It's Mrs Gentle.'

Chapter Three

I waive the quantum o' the sin,
The hazard of concealing;
But och! It hardens a' within,
And petrifies the feeling!
                    – Robert Burns

Great gusts of rain blew in from the Atlantic on the grisly scene as the body of Mrs Gentle was brought up the cliff face. Blair had arrived and was marching about over the heather on the clifftop.

'He's wiping out any clues,' muttered Jimmy.

'There won't be any footprints on this heather,' said Hamish. 'Here's the pathologist.'

Dr Forsythe arrived while a tent was being set up over the body. The men struggled with it for some time as the wind whipped it around until at last they got it firmly anchored.

Blair approached Hamish and Jimmy. His choleric eyes fell on Jimmy. 'What were you doing up here?'

43

'Day off, sir,' said Jimmy. 'Thought I'd help Macbeth look for his missing fiancée.'

'And whit made ye look ower the cliff?'

'I thought she might have been killed,' said Hamish.

'More likely to hae committed suicide at the thought o' being wed to a loon like you,' said Blair.

They all looked at the tent where, in the strong lights that had been rigged up, the shadow of the pathologist could be seen bending over the body.

Blair retreated to his car. Hamish waited anxiously. Dr Forsythe at last emerged. She went straight up to Hamish. 'It's murder, plain as day,' she said. 'She was strangled before she was thrown over the cliff.'

'What this?' demanded Blair, lumbering up. 'You should report first to me.'

Dr Forsythe looked at him with dislike. 'It's a murder. Mrs Gentle was strangled and thrown over.'

'The women cleaning the house might have seen something,' said Hamish.

'Whit women?' growled Blair.

'She had hired women from Braikie to clean up the mess after the reception. I called on her earlier today to have a look at Ayesha's room and see if she had left any clues. There was nothing. All she had is in the two suitcases she left at the police station. In one suitcase is ten thousand pounds given to her by Mrs Gentle. When Jimmy and I were here this morning, we could hear the women cleaning.'

'We'll need those suitcases. Was her passport in one of them?'

'No,' said Hamish. 'No passport.'

'Looks as if she strangled her employer and ran for it. She must have got that passport picture doctored somehow.'

Hamish stiffened. 'Why?'

'Why? Because we got a photo of the real Ayesha wired over, and she's fair but small. Get into Braikie, Macbeth. I'll send some other men as well. We've got to find thae maids.'

Hamish drove into Braikie. He stopped at a fish-and-chip shop and bought a fish for Sonsie and a meat pie for Lugs, watched while they ate, and then drove off to the council estate. He remembered that Bessie, who used to do the cleaning at the Tommel Castle Hotel, had moved to Braikie. What was her married name? Hunter, that was it. He took out his laptop and brought up the Highlands and Islands telephone directory. There were only two Hunters on the estate, a J. Hunter and an A. Hunter. He could not remember the first name of Bessie's husband, so he tried the address of A. Hunter. Bessie herself answered the door.

'Why, Hamish!' she said, looking alarmed. 'What's up?'

'Nothing to do with your family,' said Hamish. 'Can I come in?'

She stood back and he walked into Bessie's cheerful living room. 'Where's your man?' he asked.

'Andy's doing late shift at the paper works in Strathbane.'

Hamish removed his cap. 'Sit down, Bessie. This is about Mrs Gentle. She's been found murdered.'

'Oh, my God! How? Where?'

'Someone strangled her and threw her over the cliff. Now, were you working for her?'

'Aye, me and Annie Chisholm.'

'When did you finish?'

'We finished about three in the afternoon. She'd been hustling us along because she was paying by the hour. We started at nine in the morning.'

'And she was there when you left?'

'No. The phone rang. She looked quite cheerful but said she had to go out for a breath of fresh air.'

'What time would this be?'

'It would be just about after you left. I saw you drive off. That would be around eleven o'clock. She asked us how long it would take and as she wanted the bedrooms and the like cleaned as well, we told her it would be

46

around three in the afternoon. She'd been complaining about the price since the minute we arrived but she paid up the money without a murmur. I asked her if she wouldn't be back before we finished, and she said, "Maybe not. Here's the spare key. Lock the door behind you and put the key through the letter box."'

'And how did she seem?'

'Quite happy, not excited. Poor woman. Who would kill her? Is your lassie still missing, Hamish?'

'Yes.'

Bessie's round country face creased in sympathy. 'It's a right shame.'

'Where does Annie Chisholm live?'

'Round the corner. Broom Close, number ten.'

'If you can remember any little thing, let me know.'

Annie Chisholm was a short, burly woman. When she heard Hamish explain the reason for his visit, she exclaimed, 'I didnae like the woman. But this is awfy. She started off being a slave driver. The only break we got was when you arrived and then she was back, following us around. When she got that phone call, she changed. She was just too happy to pay us the money and get out.'

'No member of her family around?'

'Not a soul. She was on her own when we

were there. I tried at one point to speak to her, saying it was a shame you'd been stood up on your wedding day, and she said that it couldnae have happened to a nicer fellow, sneering, like. I could hardly believe my ears because everyone in Braikie thought she was some kind of a saint what with paying for the wedding and all.'

'She didn't say anything about the missing girl?'

'Not a word. She still missing?'

'Aye.'

'She get on well wi' Mrs Gentle?'

'As far as I know,' said Hamish abruptly.

When he left, he realized that Ayesha, or whoever she was, might turn out to be the prime suspect.

He drove back to the police station, where he filed a long report of the finding of the body and of his interviews with the two cleaners. When he finally got to bed with his cat at his side and his dog at his feet, he somehow became more and more convinced that his fiancée was dead.

In the morning, Superintendent Daviot gave a press conference. Only a few of the local papers turned up. But as soon as he described the murder of Mrs Gentle and the missing Russian girl who had been using someone else's passport, the news flew out around the country.

Soon the press dug up the story of Hamish's failed wedding, and Hamish fled the police station with flashes going off in his face to escape their questions. Earlier that morning, Jimmy had turned up with a forensic team who had gone over the luggage and then taken it away. Before leaving, Jimmy had said the family were travelling up to the castle.

Hamish did not fear being hounded by Blair because Blair was jealous of him and would want the whole case to himself. He felt sure that if 'Ayesha' were safe somewhere, then someone in the Highlands must have seen her. She was too tall and beautiful to escape attention.

When he reached Braikie, Jimmy phoned him. 'Got the news over from Istanbul police,' he said. 'Your girl was called Irena Selakov from Moscow. Top hooker. Protector was a Russian businessman, runs a chain of restaurants in Moscow, name of Grigori Antonov. They were visiting Istanbul on business for a week when Irena did a bunk. Russian police so far uncooperative. Say of course they'll help and then probably hope we'll forget about it. But Grigori is definitely in Moscow.'

Hamish thanked him and rang off. Most of that morning, he walked in and out of shops in Braikie, asking if anyone had seen Irena but meeting up with a blank wall everywhere, although everyone he spoke to was anxious to help, regarding him as a desperate lovelorn man, looking for his fiancée.

He drove up to the castle. The coal-mine owner who had built it had wished to copy Balmoral on a very small scale for his summer holidays. It had stood empty for some time. Hamish wondered if anyone would buy it. Who on earth would want to live in such a wild, remote spot on the edge of the cliffs, particularly with the British coastline crumbling bit by bit each year?

The rain had gone but the wind still blew and the air was full of the smell of salt. The castle door stood open. The forensic van stood outside. There was no proper fencing around the acreage belonging to the castle, only a crumbling dry-stone wall. But there were police on duty at the entrance to the drive leading up to the castle, and for the moment they were keeping the press at bay.

Hamish struggled into the coverall blue plastic suit which was now regulation for policemen visiting a possible crime scene. He walked in and stood in the hall. He wondered if they had looked in the cellars yet. He could hear them moving about upstairs. He went into the kitchen. There was a rack inside the door holding keys. Putting on a pair of latex gloves, he selected one marked cellar and then searched around the hall until he saw the cellar door.

He unlocked the door and groped around at the top of the stairs until he found a light switch. He went down into the cellar. Down here, he could hear the boom, boom, boom of the waves.

There were a few racks of wine in dusty bottles. In the centre of the cellar was a wooden table which held a bottle and two glasses, one clean and one dirty. He sniffed at them and then sniffed the air. There was a faint smell of vomit. He looked down at the stone floor. It was clean. He turned and looked back at the stairs; they looked clean as well. He walked around the wine racks. Several large trunks were piled against the wall. He turned and climbed up the stairs, searching the rooms until he found the chief forensic officer, Bruce Murray.

'Look, Bruce,' said Hamish. 'I've been down in the cellar. I swear it's been cleaned recently, and there's a faint smell of vomit. Now, there are some old trunks there, and I don't want to get into trouble for compromising a crime scene. Would you mind taking your team down there and opening up those trunks?'

'Why?'

'There might be a body in one of them.'

'You've been looking at too many horror movies.'

'Okay. If I find anything and get a rocket, I'll say you refused to search.'

'Oh, all *right*! But I'll do it myself.'

He followed Hamish down to the cellar. The first trunk was empty, the second held fusty old clothes, a third, children's toys and books, and the fourth old accounts and letters. The fifth at the bottom, a huge old steamer trunk, was pulled out, Bruce grumbling all the time. Hamish undid the old leather straps and threw back the lid.

'Will ye look at that,' marvelled Bruce. 'You're psychic.'

'That' was the dead body of Irena, doubled up and crushed into the trunk.

Her blonde hair was matted with blood. Hamish took out his phone. 'Can't get a signal down here,' he said. 'I'll go upstairs.'

'I'll wait for the pathologist and then get the boys down here,' said Bruce. 'Do you know Dr Forsythe is leaving the force?'

'Why?'

'She wants to retire. Besides, she says that a forensic pathologist here only earns a third of what they do in England. Don't know where we'll find another. Probably need to get someone all the way from Aberdeen.'

Hamish went upstairs. He felt numb. He phoned Jimmy, not wanting to hear Blair's bullying voice. Then he walked outside the castle and stood waiting. He suddenly craved a cigarette. He had stopped smoking some time ago, but occasionally the longing would come back.

Was there a serial killer on the loose? Had some maniac come to the Highlands?

He discounted any Russian connection. Whoever had phoned Mrs Gentle had been someone she knew. She had happily gone out to meet whoever called her. Perhaps Irena had just got in the way. But wait a bit – Irena had been killed *before* Mrs Gentle was strangled and thrown over. He was sure of it.

The gale blew the sound of approaching sirens. Jimmy arrived with Detective Constable Andy MacNab. In the following car came more detectives, a vanload of police after them.

'Where's Blair?' asked Hamish.

'In the hospital with alcohol poisoning. How that man can keep on going is beyond me. So what have we got?'

Hamish told him briefly about finding the body. 'The press are going to have a field day,' said Jimmy when Hamish had finished. 'Here comes Dr Forsythe. I'll hae a look at the body when she's finished. How do you feel?'

'I don't know,' said Hamish. 'Stunned, I guess.'

Dr Forsythe got out of her car. 'Where's the body?'

'Down in the cellar. I'll take you there,' said Hamish.

'Did she have any scratches on her face?'

'Too much blood,' said Hamish. 'Why?'

'Despite being in the water, Mrs Gentle had fragments of skin under her fingernails. I'm working on the DNA.'

'Do you think Irena killed her and then struck herself on the head with a hammer in a fit of remorse?'

'Don't be cheeky, Hamish. I only meant that there's hope the person who killed her might be on the DNA database.'

'Here's the cellar,' said Hamish. 'You'll find Bruce down there.'

'Sober, I hope.'

'For the moment.'

Hamish went back and joined Jimmy. 'What's odd,' he said, 'is that on a table in the cellar is a bottle with two glasses. Almost as if someone had lured Irena down there, given her a drugged drink, and then bashed her head in.'

'What? On the morning of her wedding? Mrs Gentle said she went out for a walk.'

'Have you checked the phone records?'

'Yes. That phone call to Mrs Gentle came from a call box in Lochdubh. Any strangers in Lochdubh?'

'I suppose there are visitors up at the Tommel Castle Hotel.'

'Her family are due to arrive today,' said Jimmy. 'What a mess. You'd best get down to Lochdubh and ask around. Put a sign on that phone box and some police tape around it until the forensic people see if they can get anything off the receiver. Then check who's staying at the hotel.'

'Can't I wait for the pathologist's report? You're not Blair.'

'Well, just till then.'

They waited a long time while the sky grew darker and sheets of rain began to sweep across the landscape.

At last Dr Forsythe came up from the cellar. 'She was struck a heavy blow to the head with a blunt object. I'll have a better idea of what sort of object when I get the body back to the lab. I can't tell the time of death until then, either, but from the state of the corpse it does look as if she was killed on the day of her wedding.'

'But the only person in the castle then was Mrs Gentle,' exclaimed Hamish. 'Could a wee woman like that have had the strength to get that body in the trunk?'

'I'll need to check the toxicology. There were traces of vomit in her mouth. Whoever put the

55

body in the trunk then jumped up and down on it to cram it in. Her ribs are broken. At the moment, mind you, that's just a guess.'

'Off you go, Hamish,' said Jimmy.

Hamish turned to go and then stopped, poised on one foot like a heron.

'What now?' asked Jimmy.

'Can you let me know what Mrs Gentle's background is?' asked Hamish. 'I mean, her maiden name, who she was married to, all that?'

'Look, I'll drop in on you later.'

As Hamish hung a sign on the phone box saying it was not to be used, he noticed that the light inside the old-fashioned red box had been smashed. He put police tape around it. When he started, there hadn't been a soul on the waterfront, but when he finished he found that a small crowd had gathered. Archie Maclean, the fisherman, was there. 'We're right sorry to hear about your poor fiancée,' he said.

'How did you find out?'

'Gamekeeper Diarmuid heard it frae his cousin in Braikie who got it frae Ellen, the cousin's sister, who got it frae –'

'Oh, all right, Archie. It's a sad business. Did any of you see any strangers in the village yesterday?'

Mrs Wellington, the minister's wife, volunteered that several guests from the hotel had been seen in the village buying postcards. 'Would you like my husband to have a word with you, Hamish? You must be grieving. The police should have more sensitivity than to put you on this case.'

'I'm better working,' said Hamish.

'We felt a bit mean, taking all our presents back,' said Mrs Guthrie, one of the villagers. 'So Mrs Wellington told us to put them on display in the church hall and you can pick out what you need for the station.'

Hamish looked at the kind, concerned faces and turned abruptly away, a lump in his throat. 'Very kind,' he said hoarsely, and hurried off to the police station.

'Near tears, the poor soul, poor soul,' said Jessie Currie. There was a murmur of sympathy.

Hamish got into the Land Rover. He felt very low. He had a guilty feeling of relief that Irena was dead and could not come back into his life to threaten him. He also felt guilty over the villagers' warmhearted sympathy.

Priscilla Halburton-Smythe received another phone call from her father. 'You've had a lucky escape, my girl,' said the colonel. 'Hamish Macbeth has murdered that fiancée of his.'

'What?'

'Some reporter's just told me. She's been found dead in a trunk in the cellar of that folly the other woman was living in, the one who ended up at the bottom of the cliffs. Who else would want rid of her but Hamish? Folks say he looked relieved when she didn't turn up on his wedding day.'

'Don't be ridiculous. Hamish wouldn't hurt a fly. If everyone is saying what you're saying, he'll need some support. See you soon.' And, deaf to her father's protests, she rang off.

Elspeth Grant was summoned to the newsroom. 'Get yourself up to Lochdubh fastest,' said the news editor. 'Bodies all over the place. One at the foot of the cliffs and now the fiancée of that copper has been found murdered.'

'Hamish Macbeth?'

'That's the man.'

Mr Johnson, the hotel manager, welcomed Hamish cautiously. 'I'll give you a cup of coffee before you start questioning the guests. But don't go upsetting them, mind? And do you have to bring those weird animals with you? Go and put them back in your vehicle. That cat of yours is enough to scare a man to death.'

'She's just a pussycat,' said Hamish crossly,

but he put the dog and cat in the police Land Rover, leaving the engine running and the heater on.

He was just about to sit down in the manager's office when Mr Johnson said, 'I'd better go out to the car park. Someone's running their engine. Maybe I'll wait a minute and see if they drive off.'

'That's mine,' said Hamish sulkily.

'Whatever for? Oh, I know. The beasties have to be kept warm. Hamish, they are animals. They come supplied by the good Lord with coats. Go and turn that damn engine off.'

Hamish stalked out and returned shortly. 'You're a hard man,' he said, picking up his cup of coffee.

'And you're a softie. I've got news for you.'

'About the murders?'

'Not them. Wait a bit, *murders*? I thought there was only the one.'

'My fiancée who turns out to have been a Russian has been found in the cellar of the castle in a trunk with her head bashed.'

'I am so sorry. You must be feeling awful. Did you love her very much?'

'Something like that,' said Hamish hurriedly. 'What news?'

'Priscilla phoned to say she's coming up, and your friend Elspeth Grant has booked a room. She's lucky we had one left. The press are booking in as hard as they can.'

'It'll be grand to see them,' lied Hamish, who did not wish any more complications in his already complicated life. It would soon come out that Irena had been a hooker, and he knew that would shock the villagers.

'I thought your fiancée was Turkish.'

'So did I,' said Hamish. 'I'm afraid she tricked me.'

'You can't have been very close then. You're usually awfully sharp.'

'There was the rush getting the necessary permission to marry her,' said Hamish.

'I saw her,' said Mr Johnson. 'She was stunning. I can't blame you for being swept off your feet.'

'It seems that all she wanted was British nationality.'

'So that's why you don't seem to be grieving.'

Hamish finished his coffee. 'I'd better start with the guests.'

'The trouble is,' said the manager, 'a lot of them have left. The press are apt to get very drunk and noisy. There are a couple of hotels up Braikie way, as you know, and plenty of bed-and-breakfasts, but the press always want to choose the most expensive hotel.'

'Any of them seem suspicious? I mean, the guests?'

'No, all very quiet and respectable. Mostly fishing types. We've got a writer. Harold Jury.

Quite well known. His last book, *Depths of Darkness*, was nominated for the Booker Prize.'

'I'd like to start with him. Writers are supposed to observe life more than ordinary people.'

'Maybe. But this one's head is so far up his own arse, he could clean his teeth from the inside.'

'I'll try him anyway. Where is he at the moment?'

'He's probably in the lounge. He sits there with his laptop, showing off.'

Hamish strolled into the lounge. A man sat staring at a laptop. On a small table beside him was a pile of books.

'Mr Jury?'

Harold Jury held up one hand for silence and continued to type. 'I'll sign a copy of my book for you in a minute,' he said. He was tall and pale-faced, probably in his late fifties, and wearing a grey shirt with grey trousers. He had thick brown hair and small brown eyes.

'This is police business,' said Hamish loudly, 'so switch off your computer and pay attention.'

Harold glared at him but did as he was told. He looked up angrily at the tall policeman with the hazel eyes and flaming red hair.

Hamish pulled up a chair and sat facing him. 'I am investigating two murders,' he began.

'What on earth has that got to do with me?' asked Harold.

Hamish noticed that he did not ask which murders – and the murder of Irena had not yet reached the newspapers. Of course, the press in the hotel might have got wind of it already and told him.

'Were you in the village yesterday morning around eleven o'clock?'

'Yes, I took a walk. I bought some postcards.'

'Did you see anyone in the phone box?'

'I don't even remember seeing a phone box.'

'What brought you up to the Highlands?'

'I am writing a novel about the forgotten primitive people of the British Isles.'

'And do the forgotten primitive people usually run five-star hotels?'

'I must confess I am disappointed. But I shall walk out on to the moors and speak to crofters.'

'I'm sure they'll give you a right primitive welcome,' said Hamish. 'Part of the highland greeting is to strike the visitor several times with a branch before inviting him inside. Then he must swallow a small bowl of rock salt and eat a piece of dried bread.'

'I don't know if I could cope with that.'

'Try,' urged Hamish. 'In fact, you don't need to go up on the moors. Why not try the village? There's a fisherman, Archie Maclean, has the wee cottage down by the harbour. I'll tell him you're coming.'

'That's kind of you. I suppose a writer must suffer for his art.'

Hamish decided he was wasting his time at the hotel. Surely the villagers were the best bet. He called on Archie Maclean first. 'I cannae ask you in, Hamish,' said Archie. 'The wife's down in Inverness visiting her sister. She'll check when I get back to make sure I havenae dirtied anything.'

'I won't bother you,' said Hamish. 'But I want you to do something for me. It's a bit of a joke . . .'

When Hamish had finished preparing Harold Jury's highland welcome, he realized he would have to visit the Currie sisters, Nessie and Jessie, Lochdubh's spinster twins. They noticed everything that happened in the village.

He could only hope that they had not yet learned of Irena's profession.

Chapter Four

Oh, what a tangled web we weave,
When first we practise to deceive!
                    – Sir Walter Scott

Hamish parked on the waterfront and walked towards the Currie sisters' cottage. Anxious to delay going in, he stood with his back to the loch and surveyed his home village, sharply aware, not for the first time, how much he loved the place.

It was dark, and lights shone from the windows of the small whitewashed cottages. You could tell the time of day by the smells in Lochdubh, thought Hamish. Morning was redolent with bacon and eggs and strong tea, intermingling with the scent of peat smoke from newly lit fires. Then, no such thing as lunch in Lochdubh. Dinner was in the middle of the day. Complex smells of soup, beef stew, roast lamb, and again strong tea – tea with everything, and it must be nearly black in colour. High tea was at six o'clock. No one wanted newfangled oven chips. Chips must be fried in cholesterol-building lard. High tea brought the smell of kippers or sliced ham along with the sugary smell of cakes, because no high tea was properly served unless there were plain cakes and iced cakes. Supper was cocoa-and-toasted-jam-sandwiches time.

Hamish sniffed the chocolate-scented air. Suppertime already. Nine o'clock. With a sigh he approached the Curries' cottage. The door opened just as he reached it.

'We saw you hanging about across the road,' said Nessie. 'Wasting police time, that's what you were doing.'

'I need to ask you some questions,' said Hamish.

'Come ben.' Hamish followed her into the small front parlour. Jessie Currie was watching television. 'You interrupted this programme, this programme,' said Jessie, who always repeated the last words of her sentences.

'It's fair amazing the way you can keep one eye on the telly and keek out o' the window with the other,' said Hamish.

'Oh, sit down and get on with it,' said Nessie. 'Well, my lad, you had a lucky escape. A prostitute! We could hardly believe our ears.'

'Believe our ears,' echoed her sister, her eyes glued to a fornicating hippo on a wildlife programme.

Hamish sighed. They complained of leaks at Number 10; they complained of leaks at the White House. But those were nothing compared with the Highlands of Scotland, which leaked information day in and day out like a sieve.

'You ken Mrs Cullie, her what lives up the brae?'

'Aye.'

'Her niece is a nurse at Strathbane hospital and she heard that fat detective, Blair, laughing fit to burst a gut. She asked him what the matter was and when he could finish laughing he said he'd just received a phone call and learned you were about to wed a hooker.'

For once Jessie was too engrossed in the programme on television to echo her sister's comments. A wildebeest was being savaged by a pack of hyenas. Probably the producers of the programme orchestrated the kill, thought Hamish cynically.

'Forget about that,' said Hamish crossly. 'Now, yesterday morning, someone made a call from that phone box on the waterfront, around eleven o'clock. Did you see anyone?'

'Let me think. Oh, turn the sound down, Jessie. Aye, I mind I was coming out o' Patel's. He'd just got in some nice ham. I like a slice of ham at teatime. I'd got that and a can of Russian salad. What else? Oh, I know, another

67

packet of beef lard. You can't make proper chips with oil. And –'

'For heffen's sakes!' howled Hamish. 'Forget the shopping list and chust be telling me who you saw.'

'No need to shout, laddie. It was a woman, quite tall, wearing a headscarf, but she had brown hair, I could see that, and dark glasses. She was wearing a tweed jacket and shooting breeches, lovat socks and brogues on her feet. The head scarf was a red-and-gold pattern.'

Hamish wrote busily in his notebook. 'Anything about her face?'

'She had a big mole on her chin, on her chin,' said Jessie.

'That's all we could see,' said Nessie. 'Those dark glasses were so big.'

'Did you see anyone speaking to her?'

'Mrs Wellington tried to. But the woman just put her head down, got on her bike, and pedalled off.'

'On a bike? What kind of bike? Mountain bike?'

'No, it was one o' thae old-fashioned ladies' models with the basket on front. We used to call them sit-up-and-beg, didn't we, Jessie?'

But Jessie had returned to watching her wildlife programme, where the helicopter carrying the cameraman was buzzing a herd of antelope and sending them stampeding in panic.

'I'll go and see Mrs Wellington,' said Hamish, closing his notebook.

'You'd better get yourself over to the hospital for a blood test,' said Nessie.

'Why?'

'You could have AIDS.'

'I neffer slept with the lassie,' shouted Hamish.

He shook his head in bewilderment as he walked up to the manse. He should not let the Currie sisters rile him, but they always managed to.

Mrs Wellington answered the door to him. 'Come in, Hamish. I'd offer you a cup of tea but I don't want to catch one of those sexual diseases.'

'I did not even kiss her,' said Hamish grimly. 'All I want from you is a bit of information. Now, yesterday morning, the Currie sisters said you tried to talk to a tall woman who then rode off on a bike.'

'Oh, her. I was about to welcome her to the village and tell her about the church services, but she just ignored me.'

Mrs Wellington's description of the woman tallied with that of the Currie sisters. Hamish thanked her and picked up his peaked cap, which he had laid on the kitchen table. Mrs Wellington whipped a disinfectant wipe out of its packet and scrubbed the table where his hat had been lying.

Hamish sighed. The news that he had been on the point of marrying a prostitute would be all around the village, and would seep up to the Tommel Castle Hotel. The colonel would no doubt phone his daughter, Priscilla, to tell her all about it.

He collected the Land Rover and went back to the police station. He fed the dog and cat but only made a sandwich for himself. He sent over the description of the mysterious woman to Strathbane and was about to go to bed when Jimmy Anderson arrived.

'I could almost wish Blair were back on his gouty feet to take over,' groaned Jimmy. 'Daviot's decided to head the investigation himself.'

'Surely anything's better than Blair.'

'Daviot fusses and frets. Usually when he deals with the press, it's a carefully orchestrated press conference. He's not used to dealing wi' the wolf pack on the ground. The forensic lab's groaning that it's got cases a year old, but Daviot wants DNA results now. Dr Forsythe's working hard. She wants to retire after this case.'

'So how far have they got?'

'Still too early. Dr Forsythe is checking the toxicology. She thinks a big strong lassie like that might have to be drugged first.'

'I thought of that myself. But maybe if she was hit hard on the head with a hammer or something, she wouldn't need to be drugged.'

'Right. But there were no drag marks on the stairs. I know it looked as if the cellar had been recently cleaned, but something would have shown up if she'd been hit on the head and pulled down the stairs. Even cleaned-up blood shows up under those blue lights they were flashing around. So it stands to reason it was someone she knew. Two glasses on the table, one bottle, no prints. A full bottle of Amontillado. Say someone said, "I've got a good bottle of wine in the cellar. Come down and we'll drink to your wedding. You've got time."'

'Mrs Gentle said she went out for a walk.'

'Mrs Gentle could have been in on the murder.'

'I forgot to tell you. I've got witnesses to that phone call from the box,' said Hamish. 'I sent a report over.' He described the woman.

'I'll phone headquarters and get them on to it right away,' said Jimmy, going through to the office. 'They can start with that bike,' he called over his shoulder.

When he came back, he rubbed his hand over his bristly chin and yawned. 'I'll stay here the night, Hamish.'

'That's another pair of my underpants, not to mention another clean shirt,' complained Hamish. 'Want a drink?'

71

'I don't. Blair's alcoholism has given me a real scare.'

Harold Jury knocked on Archie Maclean's door the following morning. 'Your local policeman suggested I call on you,' said Harold, looking down at the small fisherman. Archie was not what he had expected. He had fondly pictured a tall, burly son of the sea, not this small man in a cloth cap and a tight suit.

'Come ben,' said Archie. 'Oh, wait a minute.' He reached behind the door, picked up a fir branch, and struck Harold across the face with it. He chanted something in Gaelic, then said, 'Now you can come in.'

The blow had been a light one, but Harold still felt shocked. He followed Archie into the kitchen. The floor was covered in newspapers. 'The wifie's house-proud,' said Archie. 'Don't want to get dirty marks on the floor.'

He placed a bowl of rock salt on the table and said, 'Eat up. Welcome to ma house.'

'Can I have some water with this?' asked Harold.

'No, the traditional highland welcome says you hae to eat it straight.'

Harold gulped and swallowed. His mouth felt as if it were on fire. At last he finished the small bowl of salt. 'What now?' he asked.

'This,' said Archie. He picked up the fir

branch and struck Harold again. 'Welcome and goodbye.'

'That's it?' Harold rose from his chair at the kitchen table.

'Aye, that's it.'

Harold went straight across the road to the bar on the harbour, where he ordered a pint of beer and gulped it down his throat. He was beginning to feel obscurely that there was something too odd about the whole business. He ordered another pint and turned away from the bar, looking for a place to sit down. He noticed that the bar seemed to have filled up, and a group of men were looking at him with covert amusement. An awful suspicion began to grow in his mind. He left his pint untouched and drove back to the Tommel Castle Hotel, where he confronted the manager and demanded to know if what he had experienced was a highland welcome. When he had finished laughing, Mr Johnson asked, 'Where did you get such a silly idea from?'

Furiously Harold described how Hamish Macbeth had sent him to see Archie Maclean. 'Do you mean it was all a joke?'

'I'm afraid so.'

'I shall report that policeman to his superiors. I shall phone the local newspaper.'

'I wouldn't do that if I were you. You'll look a right fool.'

Harold realized the truth of it. 'I'm getting out of here,' he yelled. 'Get my bill ready.'

The office door opened, and the vision that was Priscilla Halburton-Smythe walked in.

She stood in a shaft of sunlight. Her smooth blonde hair was a perfect bell. She was wearing a green wool suit. Thoughts of the fairy queen ran through Harold's head.

'Can I help?' asked Priscilla. 'I am Priscilla Halburton-Smythe.'

'It's all right,' said Mr Johnson. 'Mr Jury was just asking for his bill. Mr Jury?'

Harold was hanging on to Priscilla's proffered hand with a dazed look on his face. 'Eh, what?' he asked, as Priscilla firmly withdrew her hand. 'Oh, that.' He forced a laugh. 'Just joking. I'll be staying on for a bit. Miss Halburton-Smythe, may I offer you a drink?'

'Well . . .'

'I'm afraid I got unnecessarily upset over a joke played on me by a silly policeman.'

'Tell me all about it,' said Priscilla, and she led the author from the office and into the bar.

'I'm going to interview the family,' said Jimmy that morning.

'Who's all going to be there?' asked Hamish.

'There's daughter Sarah, and son Andrew with his wife, Kylie, their two children, John and Twinkle –'

'And *what*?'

'Believe it or not, Twinkle is her name. There's also a nephew, Mark Gentle.'

'Take me with you,' urged Hamish.

'Well, sit in a corner and keep your mouth shut.'

Mrs Gentle had had the speech and manners of an upper-class lady. Her daughter, Sarah, although tall and rangy, had the same accent as her mother – the result of a good finishing school in her late teens. Andrew Gentle and his wife, Kylie, came as a surprise. Andrew was stocky and very hairy. His thick brown hair grew low on his forehead and he had hair on the back of his hands, making them look like paws. He was wearing an open-necked shirt displaying a great tuft of chest hair. His accent showed traces of cockney. Kylie was tall and anorexic-thin. She had a stiff, expressionless face – Botox, thought Hamish – and masses of artificially red hair. Her vivid blue eyes were the result of contact lenses. Her unexpectedly generous breasts, revealed by a low-cut blouse, hung on her skeletal figure like ripe fruit on a withered tree. Her accent was highland – or maybe more island, decided Hamish after listening carefully. Although soft, it held the fluting tones of the Outer Hebrides.

Andrew, it transpired, was fifty years old and his wife, forty-eight.

Daughter Twinkle was twenty-five. She had a classy accent, but that was the only thing classy about her. She had inherited her father's stocky figure. Her skin was sallow, her eyes brown, and her large mouth set in a perpetual pout.

Son John was twenty-three, tall, willowy, and effeminate. He had dirty-blonde hair worn long. His voice was pleasant but was marred by a faint lisp. Hamish noticed that he looked frightened.

Nephew Mark Gentle had a London accent. He was handsome in a rugged way: well built with a good head of blonde hair and clear grey eyes. His hands were red and callused. Hamish wondered what he did for a living.

Jimmy said he would interview them one at a time, starting with Andrew, and asked if there was a suitable room. Andrew suggested the study.

Jimmy, flanked by Andy MacNab, was to conduct the interview. A policewoman was there to take notes, even though the interviews were to be recorded. Hamish sat in a corner of the study and looked around with interest.

He doubted whether Mrs Gentle had ever used the room. It had a masculine flavour. There was a large Victorian desk and several hard chairs. Sporting prints hung on the walls;

a stuffed fox snarled in its glass case on a cabinet by the window. The room was very cold.

Jimmy shivered. 'Before we begin the questioning, Mr Gentle, is there any way of heating this room?'

Andrew left and came back with an old-fashioned two-bar electric heater decorated with fake coals on the top and plugged it in.

'How is the rest of the place heated?' asked Hamish.

'Coal fires in the rooms,' said Andrew.

But not in Irena's, thought Hamish.

Glaring at Hamish, Jimmy began the questioning. He already had in front of him a list of names, ages, and addresses. After the usual preliminaries for the tape recorder, he began. Where had Andrew been during the last week? Andrew said he had been at his office in the City of London.

'You visited your mother for a family reunion,' said Jimmy. 'What was that all about?'

'She wanted to discuss her will. It was very straightforward: half to me and half to my sister, Sarah.'

'Was your mother afraid of anyone?'

'No.'

'Did you speak to the girl we now know as Irena when you were here?'

'Of course. She was the hired help. I'd ask her to fetch me a coffee, things like that.'

'What time did she get off?'

'I don't know. Sarah'll probably know. She was staying here before Mother turfed her out.'

'When you were here, are you sure nothing was said to upset or frighten your mother in any way?'

'Not a thing,' said Andrew.

Lying, thought Hamish.

Jimmy persevered with a few more questions and then asked Andrew to send his wife in.

Kylie tottered in on her very high heels. She crossed her legs, letting her skirt ride up. The room was still cold, and her nipples stood out sharply against the thin fabric of her blouse.

No bra. Boob job, thought Hamish. Proud of it, too. Would rather die of cold than cover them up.

'Now, Mrs Gentle . . .'

'Call me Kylie.'

'Your accent sounds local. Are you originally from around here?'

'I was brought up in South Uist.'

'And how did you meet your husband?'

'I got out of South Uist as soon as I could and got a job as an air hostess. I met Andrew when he was on a business flight to the States.'

'Think carefully, Kylie. Was there anything at the family reunion to upset Mrs Gentle?'

'Get one thing straight. My mother-in-law specialized in upsetting people, not the other way round.'

'Did she upset anyone?'

'All of us. Let me see, her beloved Andrew was the only one who escaped. She constantly referred to me as the stick insect, she sneered at Sarah because Sarah hadn't yet found a job and was desperate for money, she called my daughter, Twinkle, Twinkle Little Tart, she called my son a poofter, and she told Mark it was no use him hanging around, he wasn't getting any money.'

'What about the girl, Irena?'

'Treated her like a slave. I don't know why she put up with it. Quite a beauty. I think she was jealous of the girl. Margaret always was a jealous bitch. I hated her, but I didn't murder her.'

'With all these insults flying around, surely someone threatened Mrs Gentle.'

'Nobody dared. She didn't tell us the terms of the will until we were all ready to go. Everyone was frightened of not getting a penny.'

'Why should the nephew, Mark Gentle, expect anything?'

'He's Andrew's brother's boy. Couldn't make him out. You'd better ask him.'

Hamish spoke up from his corner. 'Who was Mrs Gentle married to?'

'A financier, Byron Gentle.'

'When did he die?'

'Just after Sarah was born.'

Jimmy glared at Hamish but Hamish ignored him.

'What did he die of?'

'A heart attack. That's where Ma Gentle got all her money from.'

Jimmy interrupted. 'Where were you during the past few days?'

'I was in London with my husband. We've got a live-in maid. You can ask her.'

'Thank you. Please send in Mark.'

When Kylie had left, Jimmy rounded on Hamish. 'What was the point of your questions?'

'I just wondered if there was something in the family's past that Irena had overheard, something that she thought she could blackmail someone with.'

Mark Gentle strolled in. He seemed very much at his ease.

'Were you invited to the family reunion?' asked Jimmy.

'Yes, I wouldn't have come otherwise. Aunt Margaret always had a soft spot for me.'

'And yet she left you nothing in her will.'

'As a matter of fact, she did.'

'But we understand that she was leaving her money equally divided between her son and daughter.'

Mark gave a lazy smile. 'That was her intention. But the old will still stands, and in it I get a whack of money.'

'Do the rest of the family know this?'

'I shouldn't think so. Aunt Margaret confided in me a lot.'

'We'll check with her lawyer,' said Jimmy. His foxy blue eyes narrowed. 'You must have been right put out when you learned you were going to be cut out.'

He shrugged. 'Didn't bother me. I've always worked for my living.'

'As what?'

'Motor mechanic.'

'I gather that your late uncle, Byron Gentle, was extremely wealthy. Is your family wealthy also?'

'Dad's dead. He ran a corner shop. When Byron died, he left everything to Aunt Margaret.'

'That must have caused a lot of bitterness.'

Again that shrug. 'Mum was dead. Dad didn't live long enough to get bitter. He got cancer shortly after Byron died. I sold the shop and set up my own garage doing car repairs.'

'Why do you think Mrs Gentle changed her mind about leaving you any money?'

'Blessed if I know.'

'Were you fond of your aunt?'

'I admired her. She was very cunning. Do you know, she was a cloakroom girl in a London nightclub when Byron fell for her? She didn't always have that lady-of-the-manor act.'

Jimmy looked down at his notes. Mark was forty-eight years old. He looked much younger.

'You look good for your age,' said Jimmy.

Mark smiled. 'Clean living and early nights.'

'Where were you during the past five days?'

'At my work. I employ two men who can vouch for me, not to mention my customers.'

'And after work?'

'I was with my girlfriend, Sharon Bentley. You can check with her.'

Jimmy pushed forward a sheet of paper. 'Write down her name and address.'

When Mark had jotted it down, Jimmy continued to question him, feeling all the time that he was being stonewalled. At last he told the man not to leave the country and dismissed him.

When the door had closed behind Mark, Jimmy said, 'Now, that one really had a motive. He bumps the old girl off and Irena finds out about it and ... No, that won't do. Irena was dead before Mrs Gentle was killed.'

A policeman put his head around the door. 'The lawyer's here.'

'Send him in.'

The lawyer introduced himself as Mr Poindexter of Poindexter, Bravos and Dunstable. He said their offices were situated in Inverness. Mrs Gentle had visited them a year previous to draw up her will.

'What were the conditions of the will?' asked Jimmy. 'And how much was she worth?'

'With this building, stock and shares, and so on, close to twenty-five million pounds.'

'And how was it to be left?'

'Fifty per cent to her son, Andrew Gentle, thirty per cent to her daughter, Sarah, and twenty per cent to her nephew, Mark.'

'Did you know she planned to make a new will, leaving her estate divided equally between her son and daughter?'

'No, this is the first I've heard of it. I learned from your superintendent that you would be wishing to see me, and so I came straight here. Perhaps I should take the opportunity to have a few words with the family if they are not too distressed.'

'I don't think any of them are grieving at all,' said Jimmy.

'Where is Mr Daviot?' asked Hamish when the door had closed behind the lawyer. 'I thought he was taking over.'

'Our Supreme Being has decided that I should do the interviews first, then he'll take over and interview them all again.'

Sounds of a screaming altercation faintly reached their ears. 'Someone's not enjoying the news about that will,' said Hamish. 'You know what is puzzling me? Twenty-five million pounds is a great deal of money, yet if Byron

Gentle was a top financier, it doesn't seem much.'

'It was at the time he died,' said Jimmy. 'Let's have the daughter in.'

Sarah erupted into the room, wild-eyed with distress. 'I want you to arrest Mark right away,' she howled. 'He's your murderer.'

'Have you any proof of that?' asked Andy MacNab, speaking for the first time.

'It stands to reason. She was going to change her will, and he would have got nothing.'

'Please sit down, Mrs . . . is it Dewar?'

'Yes, I'm divorced.'

'Where were you during the past week?'

'I was down in Edinburgh looking for a job.'

'Do you have proof of that?'

'I stayed at a rotten little bed-and-breakfast, put my name down with Jipson's employment agency in Leith Walk, and went for various interviews.'

Jimmy gave her a sheet of paper and a pen. 'Just write down where you are staying in Edinburgh and the exact address of the agency.'

Hamish spoke up from his corner. 'You must have been very angry when your mother threw you out.'

'What are you talking about? Mother was devoted to me. But I wanted my independence.'

'I overheard her telling you to get out,' said Hamish. 'It was on the day I called on your mother.'

Sarah glared at him, finished writing, and then said defiantly, 'Well, no one wants to admit to having been sent away.'

'It would be as well to stick to the truth,' said Jimmy harshly. 'You were suddenly forced into finding work. What had you done before by way of employment?'

'I married young but got divorced two years ago.'

Again Hamish's voice. 'And you blamed your mother for the divorce. What happened?'

All the truculence and defiance left Sarah, and she seemed to crumple. 'I had an affair, just a brief fling. I don't know how Mother got to know of it but she told Allan, my husband. I hadn't ever worked so I told her she owed me and she could keep me.'

'That seems a good reason for murder,' said Jimmy.

'My own mother! Don't be stupid.'

'Now, about the maid, who we now know was called Irena. Was there anything that happened at the family party that she might have overheard and used to blackmail someone?'

'No, but she caused a lot of trouble. Mark was flirting with her and so was Andrew.'

More questioning, and then she was allowed to leave.

'Now what?' asked Jimmy. 'The children, I suppose. Neither of them married. We'll have John in first.'

John Gentle drifted in and sat down opposite Jimmy.

He seemed to be thinking of something other than the interview. He gazed dreamily at the ceiling while Jimmy restarted the tape recorder and read out his name, age, and address.

'Where were you during the last five days?' asked Jimmy.

John studied his nails. Then he said, 'In my studio in London.'

'You are an artist?'

'Yes.'

'Have you witnesses?'

'My friend, Robbie. He lives with me.'

'I want you to write down his full name and also where you were in the evenings.'

John bent over the paper and began to write slowly. Hamish studied him curiously. When the family had first arrived, John had looked frightened. Not any more. He was almost too calm.

When he had finished, Hamish asked, 'Have you taken tranquillizers?'

'Oh, yes. Lots. My nerves are delicate, you know.'

The questions continued, and John answered them all in the same dreamy manner.

86

He was finally dismissed and told to send his sister in.

What a name to be cursed with, thought Jimmy, when you're a stocky, tough-looking girl. Her large, almost swollen lips were somehow unnerving.

Twinkle answered all the questions he had already put to the others with a sort of brisk efficiency. She was a computer expert and worked for a merchant bank in the City. They could check that she was at her desk the day her mother was murdered.

When she had gone, Jimmy said, 'What a mouth!'

'Trout pout,' said Hamish. 'Collagen.'

'How do you know these things?'

'I observe,' said Hamish.

'Well, observe this. We seem to have at least two motives if we can break their alibis – Sarah and Mark.'

'If it was one of the family, they'd need to have had an accomplice,' said Hamish. 'The woman who made that phone call was tall and slim.'

Jimmy's phone rang. He listened carefully and then rang off. 'Dr Forsythe's done the toxicology report. Date-rape drug in the sherry. She must have felt herself blacking out and tried to vomit the drug up. It was the blow on the head that killed her. Only one of the wineglasses had been used. The other one was clean.'

'I feel if we could solve the murder of Irena, then we could find out who murdered Mrs Gentle,' said Hamish. 'Anything about her from the Russians?'

'Not yet. They should come up with something, however. It's not as if it's political.'

'Unless her protector, Grigori, is in the mafia and the Russian mafia has links to politics,' said Hamish.

'I tell you what, Hamish. Get back down to Lochdubh and see if you can find that woman or at least the bike. I'm going to have them in again.'

Chapter Five

Like the dew on the mountain,
Like the foam on the river,
Like the bubble on the fountain,
Thou are gone, and forever!
      – Sir Walter Scott

Hamish parked at the police station, fed his hens, gave his sheep their winter fodder, and cooked up lunch for his dog and cat, all the while wondering about that bicycle.

He remembered that the hotel had some bicycles which they allowed their guests to use. He decided to go there but felt forced to leave his pets behind. The press lurking outside the police station, he was sure, would snap photos of his wild cat and a debate would start whether it was right for a police officer to have such a 'dangerous animal'.

But instead of driving straight to the hotel, he parked up on the moors above Lochdubh. He needed peace and quiet to think.

How was it that he who had always considered himself to be a shrewd judge of character should have been taken in by Irena? At first, he had been sure her distress was genuine. Add to that her beauty, and so he was taken in. Had she been on the streets of Moscow before finding her protector? He guessed that the life she had led had made her hard and tough. Men were creatures to be used. Maybe she had not intended to use him, and then on reflection she discovered she had hit on a soft target. It would mean more than a passport to her to become a married woman. It would mean respectability. Yes, he decided, she would ruthlessly use every weapon she could find to make sure it happened. She would accept Mrs Gentle's offer of money and a reception – first, surely, because she knew something about her, and second because after her treatment, she felt a desire to make the woman pay.

His thoughts turned to the mysterious phone caller. By car, she could have made the journey to the castle in about twenty minutes. By bike, very much longer. So it stood to reason that she had quickly ditched the bike somewhere outside Lochdubh, got into a car, and driven off.

So where would a stranger dump a bike on the road out of the village? She might heave it over the bridge and into the river. She wouldn't want to use a mobile phone – that could be traced. She maybe wouldn't want to drive into the village in case someone noticed the make of car and the registration number.

He drove back down to the humpbacked bridge over the River Anstey, got out, and scrambled down beside the bridge to the river.

In spring when the snow melted, the Anstey would become a raging torrent. But now it was peaceful, the golden peaty water chuckling over the rocks. And there, lying in the water, was a bicycle. He could see that the old-fashioned wicker basket on the front, described by the Currie sisters, had come partially loose and was swaying in the stream.

He telephoned Jimmy and told him of the find. Jimmy told him to guard it until the crime operatives and the forensic boys arrived.

'Is this how you go about your detecting, Hamish?' asked a cool voice from above him on the bridge. He looked up. Hair shining in the sunlight, there stood Priscilla.

His heart gave a great leap and then he reminded himself of their romance, failed because of Priscilla's coldness. How could he still hanker after a woman whose idea of lovemaking was to just lie there, supine, and suffer?

'Don't come down,' he called. He climbed up to join her. Doomed as their romance had been, there was still this warmth and trust between them. 'I've just found a bike that's part of the murder investigation.'

'You'd better get some tape,' said Priscilla. 'There's still a bunch of press outside the station, and they'll soon be along here trampling over everything.'

Hamish got police tape out of the Land Rover and with Priscilla's help began to cordon off the area.

When it was finished, Priscilla looked at him with cool blue eyes. 'Hamish, what on earth possessed you to get engaged to a tart?'

'She was beautiful, she needed rescuing, and –' added Hamish harshly – 'nobody else wanted me and I was tired of being single.'

'You broke off our engagement, not me,' said Priscilla. 'And I wouldn't go so far as to say nobody wants you.'

'What?'

'Here they come, cameras waving. And Elspeth is at the fore.'

'Look, duck under the tape and come down to the river bank,' said Hamish.

'Won't we be messing up a crime scene?'

'From the state of that bike, it was chucked over. Come on. I'll tell you all about it.'

Elspeth, penned behind the tape with the rest of the press, called down to Hamish, but he affected not to hear.

He began at the beginning, telling Priscilla everything he knew, including the destroyed passport. He had always told her everything, knowing she was trustworthy and a very good listener.

When he had finished, she said, 'How awful it all must have been for you.'

He looked at her with gratitude. No one else had thought of how he must feel.

He heard sirens in the distance. 'Are there any odd strangers up at the hotel apart from Harold Jury?'

'I'll double-check,' said Priscilla. 'I don't think so. Apart from the press, there are a few die-hard fishermen.'

Superintendent Daviot's head appeared over the parapet. 'Come up here, Macbeth, and let the men do their work. Oh, Miss Halburton-Smythe, how nice to see you.'

Priscilla and Hamish climbed up the bank. 'I'd better be off,' said Priscilla.

'Can we meet for dinner?' asked Hamish.

'I'll phone you.'

Elspeth watched them and then saw the way Hamish looked after Priscilla as she got into her car and drove off.

She edged her way back through the press and walked round to where the police Land Rover was parked on the bridge. Elspeth opened the passenger door, got in, and crouched down.

Daviot said to Hamish, 'That was good work.'

'I'm going to check at the hotel,' said Hamish. 'They've got bikes they let their guests use.'

He walked to the Land Rover, seemingly deaf to the cries of the journalists demanding to know the significance of the bicycle.

Hamish switched on the engine and then glanced down to his left and stiffened. 'Chust what do you think you are doing, Elspeth?' he demanded.

'I'm a reporter, remember? I want something to report.'

'Tell you what, if you go to the station and take Lugs and Sonsie for a walk and feed them, I'll give you something to report.'

'Like when?'

'Say five o'clock.'

'You're on, copper. What did your hooker think of the possibility of sharing a home with your two other wives – Sonsie and Lugs?'

'Get out!'

'I'm going.'

Hamish drove off, feeling highly irritated. He regretted telling Elspeth he would see her later. She had jeered at him in the past over his devotion to his pets.

When he walked into the hotel, he glanced in the bar and then walked through to the lounge not just to see if he could find any odd-looking guests, but also to see if he could meet Priscilla again.

Apart from Harold Jury and his laptop, there were no other guests in the lounge. But the surprise was that Harold appeared to be entertaining Mrs Wellington and the Currie sisters. Hamish ambled over to join them despite a ferocious keep-out-of-this look on Mrs Wellington's face.

Harold wanted to berate Hamish over the trick he had played on him, but bit his lip when he realized how silly it would make him sound.

Nessie Currie said, 'If you behave yourself, Hamish, there might even be a part for you.'

'A part in what?' Hamish asked curiously.

'The Mothers' Union is going to put on a production of *Macbeth* and we are here to ask this distinguished author to help us.'

'Has Mr Jury any knowledge of the theatre?'

'He is a cultured man, cultured man,' said Jessie. 'Which is mair than what you are. Go and find your murderers, murderers.'

Harold had been about to refuse, but the thought of becoming a presence in the village would wipe out his humiliation. From the look on the constable's face, it would irritate him no end.

Hamish walked back to the reception area. Priscilla was just coming out of the manager's office.

'Hello again,' she said. 'You look upset.'

Hamish told her of the offer to Harold. 'It's not fitting. The man could be a murderer.'

'Hamish, he is a famous author. That was a dirty trick you played on him. Fortunately I was able to soothe him by telling him you were by way of being the village clown.'

'Priscilla! That's an awfy harsh thing to say.'

'I had to do something. The press will soon leave, and the hotel needs all the guests it can get. Having someone of Jury's stature here is good for business.'

'Why? Is business that bad?'

'The European Union's lousy economy and the weak dollar are killing off the tourists. In the grouse season, we used to get the French, and Americans in the fishing season. Now most of our guests, such as we have, are home-grown. We swore that next time the press arrived in Lochdubh, we would turn them away, but we can't do that because we need the business.'

'What about the Irish? They've done well out of the Union.'

'We got one Irishman here, but he's only interested in hill walking.'

'What's his name? You didn't tell me about him.'

'It slipped my mind. Patrick Fitzpatrick.'

'What's he like?'

'Tall beanpole of a fellow. Very quiet. Courteous. Quite good-looking.'

'I'd like to look at the shed where you keep the bikes.'

'Most of them are falling to bits. Any keen cyclist usually stays at a youth hostel. The ones we get either drive or walk. I'll get the key.'

Hamish waited. Mrs Wellington's voice suddenly boomed from the lounge, 'All the perfumes of Arabia will not sweeten this little hand.'

And Harold's amused cry of, 'Splendid.'

The bastard's going to treat the whole thing as a joke, thought Hamish.

Priscilla came out with the key. They walked together out of the hotel and round to the shed where the bikes were kept. Hamish examined the lock. 'It hasn't been forced, but it's a simple lock, easily picked. Did Johnson say anything about anyone asking for a bike?'

'Yes, just one. A Mrs Fanshawe. But she's so deadly respectable, it couldn't be her.'

'I've got to meet her.'

Priscilla opened the door and they went into the dusty darkness of the shed. 'Mr Johnson said she borrowed the mountain bike. We've only two of them. The rest are pretty old.'

'And shoogly,' said Hamish. 'You're right. Half of them look as if they would fall to bits.'

'Yes, but the thing is, Hamish, I can't

remember us having a bicycle like the one in the river.'

She went over to straighten a bike which had fallen, but Hamish said, 'Don't touch it. Might be an idea to get this place dusted for fingerprints. Let's go back to the hotel. I'd like to meet this Mr Fitzpatrick.'

'He usually turns up about now for afternoon tea.'

Hamish's stomach rumbled. He had not yet had time to eat anything. 'Is there any hope of tea for me?' he asked. 'I'm awfy hungry.'

'You don't change,' laughed Priscilla. 'All right. Mr Fitzpatrick is a bit cheap. I'll offer to pay for his tea and order one for you.'

Patrick Fitzpatrick was delighted to accept Priscilla's offer of afternoon tea. He was a slim, fit-looking man in his forties with a shock of ginger hair, a thin face, a small pursed mouth, and skin reddened by walking in the cold.

Priscilla said, 'Mr Fitzpatrick –'

'Patrick, please.'

'Very well. Patrick. Hamish Macbeth here would like to ask you a few questions.'

He paused, a scone dripping butter in his hand. 'What could I possibly know that could help the police?' His Irish accent was light, and his voice unexpectedly high and reedy.

Hamish gulped down a tea cake and asked,

'You do a fair bit of walking. Have you seen a strange woman around? She's tall, possibly wearing dark glasses, headscarf, breeches.'

'Oh, her,' said Patrick, reaching out for another scone.

'Where?' asked Hamish urgently. 'Where did you see her and when?'

'It must have been the day before yesterday. I was walking along the upper reaches of the river, must have been about two o'clock. She was coming the other way. I shouted out, "Fine day", but she stared at me for a moment and then turned and hurried off up the brae. Then I heard the sound of a car starting up.'

'Can you remember exactly at which point on the riverbank you saw her?'

'It's where the river makes a loop and there's a stand of silver birch.'

'I know it. I'd better go and have a look.' Hamish grabbed two tiny sandwiches and hurried off, eating them as he went. He realized he would need to go back at some point and ask Patrick what he did for a living and why he was at the hotel.

He drove up into the hills and followed the narrow one-track road which ran along beside the River Anstey. He parked on the road above the bend in the stream described by Patrick and looked around. He searched the road, then went down and searched along the river. He had recently seen a detective series on television where the detective had found a book of matches with the name of a sinister nightclub. The only things he found were two rusty tin cans.

The nights were drawing in. He looked at his watch. It was just coming up to five o'clock. He'd better get back to the station.

He found not only Elspeth but also Jimmy waiting for him. 'There's no time to talk to your lady friend,' said Jimmy. 'We've got to get down to headquarters. Some Russian detective's come over.'

'I didn't think the death of a prostitute would rank high on their list of investigations.'

'It's an inspector called Anna Krokovsky. She's been visiting the Met in London to study British police methods. She read about our case in the newspapers and asked to be sent north. You're to come with me to headquarters.'

'I'm sorry, Elspeth,' said Hamish. 'I'd better go. But you've got a wee bit of a story.' He turned to Jimmy. 'I don't suppose there'll be anything wrong in Elspeth writing about her visit?'

'Shouldn't think so, Hamish. Come on.'

'I'll lock up when I go,' said Elspeth. Her laptop was on the kitchen table.

'Right. Put the key back up on the gutter. What's this Russian woman like?'

'Don't know. Haven't met her yet. I only just got the summons.'

Does anyone still drink sherry? wondered Hamish as Helen, Daviot's secretary, tried to whip a tray of glasses past him so that he couldn't have any – without success, as Hamish had long arms. But then, the murderer had tempted Irena with Amontillado.

Daviot was beaming. He was at his most avuncular. 'This pretty lady has come to watch our methods. Inspector Krokovsky, may I present the detective at the moment leading the investigation with my help – Detective Inspector Jimmy Anderson. Then there is Detective Sergeant Andy MacNab and now our local constable, Hamish Macbeth.'

Anna Krokovsky nodded and sipped her glass of sherry. She was of medium height with a face that somehow reminded Hamish of Putin. Her grey eyes were watchful and her trim body, in a well-tailored uniform, slight but muscular. Her hair was her one beauty, being very thick, wavy, and dark brown.

'Perhaps,' said Daviot, 'you would like to say a few words, Miss Krokovsky.'

101

'It's Inspector Krokovsky,' she said. 'I took this opportunity to investigate policing in the provinces, particularly as the investigation concerns one of our nationals.' Her English was obviously fluent and carried faint tones of an American accent.

Hamish's highland curiosity overcame him. 'Is that an American accent, ma'am?' he asked.

'I studied at Harvard Business School before I entered the force,' she said.

'So what can you tell us about Irena?' pursued Hamish.

'Irena ran away from an orphanage in Moscow and lived on the streets. She was subsequently employed in a brothel, a top-class brothel, which is where she met her protector, Grigori Antonov. She travelled with him on business and, as you now know, stole a passport while they were in Istanbul and escaped.

'You are Hamish Macbeth. You were engaged to be married to her. I would like to speak to you as soon as possible. Where is your office? Here?'

'No, ma'am. In Lochdubh, a village about half an hour from here.'

'Is that near this castle?'

'Yes.'

'Yes what, Hamish,' barked Daviot.

'Yes, ma'am.'

'Then I would like to make a start. You will

take me to your police station and we will talk on the road.'

'It's getting late, Inspector,' said Daviot. 'Would you not like to wait until the morning?' He cast his eye over the trays of canapés. Helen would just need to parcel them up, and he could take them home.

'I would like to go now.'

Hamish fumbled for the key in the gutter, hoping that Elspeth had left, and heaved a sigh of relief when his fingers closed on it. Anna, who had driven in her own car, stood behind him and remarked, 'You are not very security-conscious.'

'Oh, no one steals anything here,' said Hamish.

He ushered her in. The kitchen was warm. Elspeth had lit the stove. Lugs and Sonsie came running to greet him.

'That is an odd cat, like a lynx,' said Anna. 'Is it safe?'

'Yes.'

She took off her huge peaked cap and placed it on the table.

'Before we begin, ma'am . . .'

'You may call me Anna when we are not officially on duty.'

'Very well, Anna. I am very hungry and I'm sure you haven't had time to eat anything.

There is a very good restaurant here. Please let me take you for dinner.'

'I would like that.'

'Oh, I forgot. You are in your Russian uniform, and there are still a number of press about.'

'I have my suitcases in my car. I will bring them in and change.'

Hamish changed into a suit, collar, and tie while Anna was in the bathroom. He had helped her carry in two huge suitcases. One lay open on his bed.

Anna eventually appeared wearing black velvet trousers, a white silk blouse with a low neckline, and a black velvet jacket encrusted with gold embroidery. Pay must be good in Moscow, thought Hamish. She went into the bedroom, opened the other suitcase, and dragged out a sable coat, which she put on.

'I am ready,' she said.

To Hamish's relief, the restaurant was quiet. 'You should ha' been here earlier, Hamish,' said the waiter, Willie Lamont. 'So many folk! Your lady is new to the village?' He hovered hopefully.

'Just give us a couple of menus, Willie, and go away,' said Hamish.

Willie came back with the menus. 'Would you like some vodka?' asked Hamish.

'I will take some wine.'

'Would that be an American accent?' asked Willie.

Anna turned pale eyes up to him. 'You are a waiter, are you not? So wait. Do not ask impertinent questions.'

When Willie had gone off again, Hamish said awkwardly, 'You must forgive Willie. He used to work for me but he fell in love with the restaurant owner's daughter. This is a very democratic village. You see, in the Highlands, everyone considers himself equal to everyone else. There are few class distinctions. If, for example, I considered myself superior to the villagers in any way, they would not gossip to me – and in the past that gossip has helped me solve cases.'

'I looked up your file,' said Anna. 'You have had a lot of success and yet you are still a village policeman.'

'I am not ambitious. I love this village. I do not want to leave.'

'Odd. Let us choose what we are going to eat.'

Hamish, mindful of his budget, settled for minestrone followed by spaghetti Bolognese. Anna chose a dish of antipasti and then an escalope Milanese.

Willie came up again and asked them stiffly what they wanted to order. This time Anna smiled at him. 'I am not American. I am Russian.'

Willie looked alarmed. 'Might I be having a wee word with you, Hamish?'

'This lady is an inspector in the Moscow police,' said Hamish, sure that Willie thought he had hitched up with another hooker.

Willie's face cleared. 'Welcome,' he said. 'I thought –'

'Never mind what you thought, Willie. Take the orders.'

When they were alone again, Anna said, 'Now, tell me how it was that you came to propose marriage to Irena.'

Hamish explained how he had thought he was doing a good turn. And then over the rest of the meal, he outlined what he knew about Mrs Gentle and how he was sure that Irena had overheard something at the family reunion that had made her a danger to someone.

'We will start first thing in the morning,' said Anna. She looked over Hamish's shoulder. A strikingly beautiful blonde woman was staring in the window at them with a look of dismay on her face.

'I'd better take you up to the hotel and find you a room,' said Hamish.

'No need. I am used to roughing it. I will sleep at your station.'

Anna looked again but the beautiful woman had gone.

Priscilla hurried back along the waterfront to the police station, where she had left her car. On impulse, she took down the key from the gutter over the kitchen door, unlocked the door, and went in. She looked in the bedroom. She looked at Anna's cases on Hamish's bed. Anna had hung away her uniform in Hamish's wardrobe.

Priscilla left and shut the door behind her. For the first time she thought that she did not really know Hamish.

She saw that bright little picture in her mind again – Hamish in his best suit talking intently to a woman as if she were the only thing that mattered in his world.

Chapter Six

*'Reeling and Writing, of course, to begin
with,' the Mock Turtle replied, 'and the
different branches of Arithmetic – Ambition,
Distraction, Uglification and Derision.'*
                                    – Lewis Carroll

Hamish received a phone call from Jimmy
early next morning, asking him to bring Anna
to the castle.

'Daviot was worried when she didn't turn
up at her hotel in Strathbane last night, but
then she phoned and said she was staying
with you. Our boss hopes you're not carrying
any détente further than it should go.'

'I've been sleeping in the cell,' grumbled
Hamish. 'I've got to get her to the Tommel
Castle Hotel this morning, somehow, and then
I'll bring her over.'

He heard a loud scream from the bedroom
and a shout of 'Get off!'

'What are you up to?' asked Jimmy.

'Nothing. She's probably found the cat in her bed.'

This turned out to be the case. Anna had awakened with the feel of a warm body stretched out next to her own.

When she was up and dressed and in her uniform, Hamish told her, 'I've taken the liberty of booking a room at the Tommel Castle Hotel. There are three people there who might interest you – Harold Jury, an author; Patrick Fitzpatrick, an Irishman; and a Mrs Fanshawe, who borrowed one of the bikes. I've yet to speak to her.'

Anna agreed. Hamish's pets had made the novelty of a stay in a highland police station quickly wear off.

'There might be some press still here,' said Hamish as he walked into the hotel with Anna, carrying her two large suitcases, 'but you'll need to face them sooner or later. While you get settled in, I'll see if I can find this Mrs Fanshawe.'

Mrs Fanshawe was having breakfast. She was a small, round, middle-aged woman with rosy cheeks and grey hair. She certainly could not have been the woman at the phone box.

In answer to his questions, she said she had borrowed a mountain bike. 'I wanted to get some of the weight off,' she said with a jolly laugh. 'One trip out was enough for me so I said to myself, Sadie, the Good Lord obviously meant you to be fat.'

She had not seen any mysterious woman. Anna walked into the dining room; at the sight of her uniform, several reporters and cameramen sprang to their feet, and soon she was surrounded. Hamish was about to interfere until he saw she was handling all questions coolly and efficiently.

When she finally said 'That's enough!' and joined Hamish, he said, 'You've only had toast for breakfast. Would you like something here?'

'No, I would like to get started.'

They met Priscilla as they were leaving the hotel. Priscilla had seen Anna only very briefly. 'Were you in the restaurant last night?' she asked Hamish when the introductions were over.

'Yes, we were going through the case.'

Priscilla smiled. Anna, with her Putin-like features, was hardly the beauty she had imagined the night before.

'Inspector Krokovsky is staying here,' said Hamish.

'Then we will do everything we can to make your stay pleasant,' said Priscilla.

When they were both in the Land Rover, before driving off, Hamish phoned his friend Angela Brodie, the doctor's wife. 'Angela, I'm going to be out most of the day. Do you think you could look after Sonsie and Lugs?'

'Hamish, you'll need to find someone to regularly take care of your pets. You're always asking me.'

'Just this once,' pleaded Hamish.

'You always say that. Oh, all right, but I've got to rehearse my part.'

'What part?'

'I rather got bullied into playing Lady Macbeth.'

'When did this happen?'

'That author held a meeting in the village hall last night. I rather got coerced into it.'

'Mrs Wellington thought she was up for the part.'

'She changed her mind.'

'Who's playing Macbeth?'

'Geordie Sinclair, the gamekeeper.'

Anna was drumming her fingers impatiently on the dashboard. 'Got to go,' said Hamish quickly.

'Are our investigations always to be delayed while you search for a sitter for your animals?' demanded Anna.

'Och, no,' said Hamish. 'All settled now.'

'Is Lady Macbeth anything to do with you?'

'It's Shakespeare. Amateur production.'

Anna settled back in the passenger seat with a sigh. In Moscow, she would have considered it well beneath her dignity to be escorted by a mere constable. She hoped the file she had read on Hamish Macbeth had not been mistaken. There was no time or place in a murder enquiry for eccentrics. And yet she had to admit to herself that there was something likeable about the man with his flaming red hair, gangly figure, and gentle hazel eyes.

'Is this a real castle?' she asked as Hamish drove up the drive.

'It's what we call a folly.'

'Does it have a name?'

'I think when it was first built, it was called Braikie Castle, but for years now it's only been known as The Folly. You can see why. It's ower-small for a castle, like a stone box with towers stuck on.'

Hamish's heart sank when he walked into the hall and saw the burly figure of Detective Chief Inspector Blair. The man must have a cast-iron liver, he thought. He introduced Anna.

'Well, Anna,' said Blair with a leer. 'What's a pretty lady like you doing up in peasantville?'

'My name is Inspector Krokovsky,' said Anna coldly, 'but you may address me as ma'am.'

Blair scowled. 'You, Macbeth, get back to your sheep. There are enough of us here.'

Anna's voice was like ice. 'Constable Macbeth is driving me. He will stay.'

Blair's temper flared up. 'May I remind you I am the senior officer here?'

Daviot loomed in the background. 'A word with you, Mr Blair, if you please.'

Jimmy came to join them. He said to Anna, 'The family are gathered in the drawing room. Would you like to meet them?'

'I would like to see where Irena's body was found first of all. Constable Macbeth can show me.'

'Is the cellar locked?' asked Hamish.

'No,' said Jimmy.

Hamish led the way. He switched on the light at the top of the stairs, and they both walked down.

'Irena's body was found in the trunk here,' said Hamish, pointing.

'And she died from a blow to the head?'

'I think it was one sharp blow. I think it was delivered by someone she knew, someone she was not afraid of.'

'That would mean a member of this family.'

'Perhaps. Unless it was someone from the time she was working in London. The castle door, as I remember, often stood open.' Hamish struck his head. 'I'm an idiot.'

'Why?'

'On the day of the wedding, Mrs Gentle was catering for the reception. There were the usual fiddly bits on trays and a bar. Knowing what I do of the late Mrs Gentle, she would not intend to pass the food round herself or serve the drinks. She must have employed a catering

114

company. No, wait a minute. If, as I believe, she was being blackmailed into holding the reception, she would want it done as cheaply as possible. I'd better get into Braikie and interview Bessie Hunter, one of the women who was cleaning up afterwards. She might know.'

'I will come with you.'

'I'd better report to Detective Chief Inspector Blair.'

'I think we will leave him for the moment. Why is this the first time I have met him?'

'He's just out of hospital.'

'What was up with him?'

'Alcohol poisoning.'

'We have that trouble with officers in Moscow. Let us go.'

Bessie Hunter was at home. To their questions, she said that she thought the catering had been done by two women, Fiona King and Alison Queen. She said they joked about themselves as being the royal caterers.

'They do the meals at the Glen Lodge Hotel outside Braikie,' said Bessie. 'But they do a bit of freelance stuff, nothing big, church socials, things like that.'

As they drove north out of Braikie towards the Glen Lodge Hotel, the road curved until it was running along beside the sea. Although the sky was blue, the heaving water had turned black. 'Storm coming,' said Hamish. 'Did you notice when we were in the cellar that the pounding of the waves seemed very close, almost as if they were thudding right against the walls?'

'I didn't notice. Why?'

'Bits of the cliffs have been falling away all along the coast. I was thinking the family won't get much for the place if they try to sell it.'

'How do you know a storm is coming?'

'Experience. When the sky is blue but the sea turns black, it usually means there's a big blow on the way.'

'Do you find this Blair creature difficult to work with?'

'Oh, dear. It could be that he doesn't like me. I am after all only a policeman, and I have only myself to blame when I am kept out of the main investigation.'

'He struck me as being stupid.'

'I really can't comment about a senior officer. Here's the hotel.'

He drove up a short drive bordered by rhododendrons and parked in front of what had once been a large private home. 'I remember this used to belong to an English family,' said Hamish, 'but the winters drove them back down south.'

'Are the winters so very bad? The air still feels quite mild.'

'Nothing like the winters in Moscow. We're near the Gulf Stream. But the wind blows a lot, and from now on we barely see daylight. It starts to get dark around two in the afternoon.'

They walked into the hotel. Hamish asked at the reception desk for Miss Queen and Miss King. They were told to wait in the lounge.

Two women in their late forties entered and introduced themselves. Fiona King was stocky with grey hair and an incipient moustache. Alison Queen was a fake blonde with a simpering manner. Both were English. They said they had always wanted to see the Highlands and had answered an advertisement for a cook. 'We always travel as a pair,' said Alison. 'The hotel said they would allow us to do some freelance work off-season.'

Hamish asked if they had seen anyone apart from Mrs Gentle when they arrived to do the catering on the morning of the reception.

'No, only Mrs Gentle,' said Alison. 'She seemed very flustered and told us we would not be wanted to serve out the canapés and drinks at the reception. She had originally said that she meant to use some of the wine from her cellar, but then she told me there was nothing down there worth bringing up.'

Fiona chimed in. Her voice had a slight lisp. 'I told her I was by way of being an expert on

wine and if she would give me the key, I'd go
down there and take a look for her. She fairly
screamed at me, didn't she, Alison pet? She
said she'd ordered drinks from the wine merchant in Braikie, and when the stuff arrived it
was the cheapest of cheap. Of course, Henry's
isn't really a wine merchant, just an off-licence,
and there was also whisky with names I'd
never heard of, cheap gin and vodka along
with the usual mixes. So we decided that she
wasn't going to waste any good wine on the
guests.'

'Did you see her Russian maid?' asked
Anna.

'The one that was to get married? No. We
assumed she was upstairs getting ready,' said
Alison.

Hamish asked, 'Was there a limousine waiting to take them to the wedding?'

'That was your wedding, wasn't it, you poor
soul,' said Alison. 'No, when we left she was
fretting, saying they would be late, but there
was only her own car outside and not even a
bit of ribbon on it, if she had meant to use
that.'

Anna asked, 'At any time you were there,
did she go upstairs to find out what was keeping Irena?'

'Come to think of it,' said Fiona, 'that's a bit
odd. She was pacing up and down, muttering
she was going to be late. Alison said, didn't

118

you, ducks, that she could run upstairs to the girl's room and find out how she was getting on, but Mrs Gentle said, "If you've finished, just go." Thank goodness we got a cheque from her there and then because we might not have got paid, considering she got shoved over the cliff.'

'And if she hadn't have been shoved over the cliff, I might have thought she killed the girl,' said Alison.

'Why did you not come forward and give the police this information?' asked Anna.

'Because we got two other jobs and put it out of our minds,' said Alison. 'I mean, when we read in the papers that Mrs Gentle had been murdered, well, we assumed that whoever killed her, killed the maid.'

'I am afraid I will have to ask you to accompany us to headquarters,' said Hamish. 'We will need to take statements from both of you.'

'Ooh! This is exciting. I'll just tell the boss where we are going.'

When they came back, they said they would follow in their own car and do some shopping in Strathbane.

'I hope it's still low tide,' said Hamish as he drove off with the cooks following, 'otherwise the shore road will be flooded.'

Great buffets of wind shook the Land Rover. Water was only just beginning to reach the

119

shore road as they drove along beside a mountainous sea.

Blair had been sent back to headquarters by Daviot, who was angry over Blair's insulting Anna. He saw them arriving and rushed down to waylay them. Anna gave him a concise report about what they had learned from the two women.

'I'll take over here,' said Blair. 'The inspector and I will take statements from these ladies. Get off wi' you.'

'I haff to drive the inspector here back to her hotel,' said Hamish.

'I'll do that. Move, laddie. That's an order.'

Blair had conducted a bullying interview and the statements had been taken. He was just leaving the police station with Anna when Daviot met them. To Blair's fury, Anna described succinctly the latest discovery and credited Hamish with finding it all out.

'And where is Macbeth?' asked Daviot.

'This man sent him away,' said Anna coldly.

'I'll have a word with you later,' said Daviot. 'Where are you off to?'

'Just taking this lady back to her hotel.'

Blair tried to converse with Anna on the road to Lochdubh, but she maintained a mutinous silence. To his surprise, though, when she reached the hotel she suddenly smiled at him.

'I think this bit of success demands a Russian celebration,' she said.

'And what's that?'

'Vodka, of course.'

Anna strode into the bar and ordered a bottle of vodka and two shot glasses. 'Now,' she said, filling up the glasses, 'we drink Russian style.'

She tossed down the contents of her glass in one gulp. Blair cheerfully followed suit. They drank toast after toast, one bottle and then another. 'And the third one ish on me,' cried Blair. He stumbled across to the bar and then was violently sick, projectile vomit which shot right across the bar and splashed on the mirror. There were a few people in the bar. They began to leave hurriedly as Blair turned round, vomited violently again, and fell on the carpet.

Priscilla came hurrying in as Anna was calmly phoning for an ambulance. 'It'll take too long to get here,' said Priscilla. But Blair was in luck. The ambulance had been in Lochdubh, delivering an elderly patient back home, when the driver received the call.

When Blair had been carried off, Priscilla said angrily, 'The man should not have been drinking at all. He was just out of hospital after a bout of alcohol poisoning.'

'Then now he has another,' said Anna. 'I must go and see Constable Macbeth.'

'Then you had better change your jacket,' said Priscilla. 'Your sleeve is soaking wet.'

'So it is. Thank you.' Anna walked off.

'She did that deliberately,' said Priscilla to the white-faced barman. 'She got him to drink and tipped most of hers down her sleeve. She could have killed him. I'd better warn Hamish. She's a dangerous woman. I'd better get the maids in here to clear this mess up. The smell is making me sick!'

Hamish was in the hen run, nailing up a board on the henhouse, when Anna arrived wearing civilian clothes.

'Your birds look quite mature,' she said. 'You do not like to kill them?'

'I keep them for the eggs,' said Hamish. 'I hear you nearly killed Blair.'

'Ah, the blonde lady who looks so sadly through restaurant windows when you are dining with another woman. She phoned you.'

'Yes, what were you thinking?'

'I was merely making an effort to be friendly. How can you think with this wind?'

'I get used to it,' said Hamish. 'I suppose people living next to the motorway get used to the sound of traffic. Must be something like that.'

'I am going back to police headquarters to find out their conclusions. The mystery must now be, if Mrs Gentle killed Irena, who then killed Mrs Gentle?'

'Could someone have followed her from Russia?'

'No one had any reason to. She was only a prostitute.'

'What about her protector?'

'An important and influential businessman such as he would not trouble himself over such a creature.'

For the first time, Hamish felt sorry for Irena.

After Anna had left, Hamish was next visited by Matthew Campbell, the local reporter for the *Highland Times*, followed by Elspeth. Matthew was in a truculent mood. 'You've been giving stories to Elspeth here when I'm your local man. I've been chasing all over the county trying to catch up with you.'

'Sit down, both of you, and I'll tell you the latest, but you've got to promise to go straight to police headquarters and get it confirmed.' He told them about the caterers' evidence and ended by saying, 'Call them before you go to Strathbane. Don't tell headquarters I said anything. Off you go. I'm tired. All I want to do is eat and go to bed.'

They stood to go, but in the doorway Elspeth turned back. Her hair was frizzy again. She had given up straightening it. Her odd silver eyes, gypsy eyes, looked at Hamish. 'Go up and see Angus, the seer.'

'That auld fraud?'

'He hears a lot of gossip.'

'Maybe in the morning, Elspeth. If I try to go up that hill to his cottage tonight, I'll get blown back down.'

Hamish chopped and fried deer liver for Lugs and cooked a trout for Sonsie and then found he was too tired to cook for himself. He had some cold chicken in the fridge. He ate it with two chopped tomatoes before having a shower and going to bed. The wind roared over the house, shrieking and yelling like a demon. He wondered just before he fell asleep why Elspeth had told him to visit Angus. But he had benefitted before from Elspeth's odd psychic experiences. Angus would want a present. Angus always expected a present. 'Silly auld moocher,' murmured Hamish and fell asleep.

He awoke early the next morning, anxious to get out of the house before Anna should reappear. Her treatment of Blair had made him uneasy. She could easily have killed the man.

But as he turned round after locking the door, he found her standing behind him.

'Maybe you'd like to go back into Braikie,' he said. 'I'm off to visit the seer. Probably a waste of time.'

'What is a seer?'

'It's a man called Angus Macdonald. He claims to see the future.'

'And you believe him?'

'No, but he picks up an awfy lot o' gossip.'

'I will come with you. I am interested.'

Hamish sighed. 'It's a bit o' a walk.'

'Then we will walk. It's a fine morning.'

The wind had abruptly died, and although the waters of the loch were still angry and choppy with yellow sunlight gilding the edges of the black waves, the sky above was blue. A gentle breeze wafted the early-morning breakfast smells to his hungry nose. He had been so anxious to escape Anna that he had not breakfasted.

He led the way up through the back of the village. 'Why *Sutherland*?' asked Anna. 'It is as far north as you can go on the British mainland.'

'It was the south land of the Vikings,' said Hamish. 'That's Angus's cottage up there.'

The cottage was perched on the top of a hill with a path winding up to it through the heather.

Angus, looking more than ever like one of the minor prophets with his long grey beard, opened the door as they arrived. 'I've been expecting ye,' he said. 'Come ben.'

'What is *ben*?' asked Anna.

'Croft houses had a but and ben. The but was where the animals lived, and the ben was where the family lived,' said Hamish.

He and Anna pulled up chairs to the peat fire. Angus sat in his rocking chair, folded his gnarled hands across his chest, and surveyed them. 'Have you something for me?' he asked.

Hamish reluctantly handed over a large packet of homemade shortbread which he had bought at a church sale.

'Ah, petticoat tails. My favourite,' said Angus. 'I'll just be putting this in the kitchen.'

'*Petticoat tails*?' asked Anna.

'The name's supposed to date from Mary Queen of Scots' time,' said Hamish. 'It's a corruption of the auld French *petit gatelles*, meaning "little cakes".'

Angus came back. He swung the blackened kettle on its chain over the fire. 'We'll have tea in a minute. So you are the Russian lady who tried to kill Mr Blair?'

'I was only having a drink with him,' said Anna stiffly. 'If he cannot hold his liquor, it is not my fault.'

'You are ruthless and hard,' said Angus. 'You would not have got the position in the

126

Russian police were you not as hard as stone. Be careful, laddie, and do not get in this lady's way.'

'Angus, when you've stopped insulting the inspector here, have you heard anything that might lead us to discover who killed Irena?'

'That would be your late fiancée who turned out to be a hooker. Dr Brodie has had to lecture the whole village on the subject of AIDS and tell them that you cannae be getting it from teacups and the like. O' course, now that you know she wass killed by her boss, you wonder who killed *her*.'

'How did you get that information?' asked Hamish angrily. 'We only knew ourselves yesterday, and as it happens we're still not quite sure that she actually killed Irena.'

'I see things. The kettle's boiling. I'll get the cups.'

'Angus, we don't want tea. We want information.'

Angus closed his eyes. Anna glared at him and half made to rise. Then Angus crooned, 'You haff to look in Mrs Gentle's past. There iss something in there the whole of her family don't want you to know.'

He opened his eyes again. 'That's it,' he said briskly.

'That's it?' echoed Hamish. 'I could ha' guessed that one myself. Come on, Anna.'

Angus's pale grey eyes fastened on Anna. 'He will be the bachelor until the end of his days.'

'This old fool knows more than he is telling,' said Anna wrathfully, and they left the cottage. 'Let's get him into an interview room and get it out of him.'

'We don't use the rubber truncheons up here,' said Hamish. 'Angus was aye a good guesser.'

As they walked back down the hill, Hamish looked fondly down at the village, *his* village, lying placidly in the sunlight, and wished with all his heart he could get rid of Anna. Her foreignness, her very ruthlessness, was upsetting him.

Chapter Seven

What bloody man is that?
– William Shakespeare

Back at the castle, Anna met the members of the family. Andrew Gentle was furious. 'We have been questioned and questioned. I do not feel like going over it again.'

The drawing room in which the members of the family were gathered was cold. Outside the narrow windows, the sun shone bravely down, but not a ray of it penetrated into the gloom.

Jimmy Anderson said, 'We are going to question you all separately again, and not because of the presence of this Russian police inspector, but because of a new development in the case. We will use the study again. Mr Andrew Gentle, you first.'

Hamish caught Jimmy by the sleeve. 'I'd be better off trying to find out something else.'

'Don't you want to see how they react to the

possibility that their mother might have killed Irena?' muttered Jimmy.

'There are enough of you,' said Hamish. 'I'll be off.'

Outside, he took great gulps of fresh air. Anna's treatment of Blair still upset him.

He decided to go to the hotel and interview the Irishman again. It was nearly lunchtime. His stomach rumbled.

At the hotel, he went round to the kitchen door. Clarry, the chef, hailed him with delight. Like Willie Lamont, Clarry had worked for Hamish during one of the brief times when Hamish had been elevated to sergeant. If he were ever to be given help again, Hamish wondered if that newcomer would also suddenly discover a yen for the catering trade.

'Any hope of a bite to eat?' asked Hamish.

'Sit yourself down, man, at that wee table by the door and keep out o' the way. I've the lunches to get ready. Soup and a sandwich do ye?'

'That would be grand.'

Clarry had three new Polish girls working for him. He complained that the trouble about Poles was that they took any job going, perfected their English, and then moved up the job ladder as quickly as possible – which meant right out of his kitchen.

The soup was cock-a-leekie, warm and nourishing. Hamish turned over the idea of Mrs

130

Gentle being a murderer in his head. She had very much wanted to appear a grand and charitable lady. He was sure her image had meant a lot to her. He would need to forget about his newfound dislike of Anna and ask her to contact Scotland Yard to get someone to dig into Mrs Gentle's background. He thought the Yard might be more likely to want to please her than Strathbane police headquarters.

When he had finished the plate of egg salad sandwiches which had been served with the soup, he thanked Clarry and went into the dining room in search of Patrick Fitzpartrick.

He noticed that Priscilla and Harold were dining together. They seemed to be getting along very well, and that surprised him. He had found Harold a pompous bore, but the man seemed to be entertaining Priscilla nicely.

He realized the other diners were all staring at him as he stood in the doorway. There was no sign of Patrick. He retreated and asked at the desk if Patrick was in the hotel; he was told that the man had taken a packed lunch and gone out walking.

And then he turned and saw Elspeth. She was wearing an Aran sweater and jeans, with her frizzy hair screwed up in a knot on top of her head.

'Get on to those caterers, did you?' he asked her.

'Let's go outside,' said Elspeth. 'It's a grand day.'

They stood together in the forecourt. 'I think they told us pretty much what they had told you,' said Elspeth, 'but it was certainly enough to make a story. Most of the other press have left, but I'm sure my story will bring them running back.'

'If she killed Irena,' said Hamish, 'it must have been because Irena had found out something that Mrs Gentle did not want known. I wonder if her husband really did die of a heart attack.'

'I researched that. Seems to have been okay. He was being treated for heart disease. Due for a bypass operation just before he died.'

'Before she met him, she was a cloakroom girl. Find anything about that in your research?'

'No, because she married Byron Gentle before he made his millions. He was a grammar school boy who got a scholarship to Oxford. After leaving Oxford, he passed his stockbroker exams and started work in the City. He seems to have been very gifted. He married her while he was still studying for his exams. Where's the Russian?'

'Up at the castle wi' Jimmy, grilling the folks. I'm right off her.'

'Why?'

'Blair got on the wrong side of her, so she

took him into the bar here and plied him with so much vodka that he got another attack of alcohol poisoning. She could have killed him.'

'Wouldn't be any great loss if she had,' said Elspeth. 'Lochdubh's abuzz with another murder.'

'What?'

'The production of *Macbeth*. They've all gone stage-mad. Matthew has even volunteered to play Banquo's ghost. Of course, there aren't many parts for women – only the three witches and Lady Macbeth.'

'Angela's playing Lady Macbeth, I know that. Which ones are playing the three witches?'

'The Currie sisters and Mrs Wellington.'

'Good casting.'

'You know,' said Elspeth, 'it would be interesting to know what the Gentle family talks about when they're on their own.'

'That's something we can't find out.'

'If you get me into the castle, I could hide a tape recorder somewhere.'

'Not on your life. This is becoming a police state. We've got more CCTV cameras in Britain than any other country in the world. I think Lochdubh must be one o' the last places without one.'

'I bet you wish they did have one,' said Elspeth. 'Then you might have seen who made that phone call, the one you've been asking everyone about.'

'Here's Mr Fitzpatrick,' said Hamish as the tall Irishman limped into the forecourt. 'I've got to ask him a few questions.'

'You again!' said Patrick. 'What's up? I've walked too far and want to get these boots off.'

'Just a few more questions. Thanks, Elspeth. I'll talk to you later. What do you do for a living, Mr Fitzpatrick?'

'I own a bookshop in Dublin.'

'And you are able to take a holiday from the shop?'

'I left my partner in charge.'

'On the day of the first murder, that would be September twenty-fifth, where were you?'

'I wrote it in my diary. I've got it here.' He pulled a fat little leather-bound book out of his anorak pocket and thumbed the pages. 'Here we are: *Went up into the foothills in the morning with my binoculars. Saw a capercaillie. Took a photograph. Ate lunch. Walked further but back downhill and round to the forest opposite the village. Very boring, nothing but miles of evergreens. Walked back to the hotel for tea. Fell asleep in the lounge. Woke up with the noise of the press arriving. Showered and changed. Ate dinner. Watched television. Went to bed.* There you are.'

Hamish's highland curiosity overcame him. 'That's all verra boring. Why do you bother to write it down?'

'It's a sort of *aide-mémoire*. The minute I see

those brief notes, I can conjure up the whole day.'

'Have you been near The Folly up near Braikie?'

'No.'

'Can you be giving me your name and address?'

'I've got a card here.' Once more he ferreted in the capacious pockets of his anorak until he found a small card case. He extracted one and handed it to Hamish. 'Why don't you arrest Harold Jury?'

'What for?' asked Hamish quickly.

'Being the most arrogant man on the planet. What Miss Halburton-Smythe sees in him is beyond me.'

'Likes him, does she?'

'Well, they've always got their heads together.'

Hamish walked into the hotel in a thoroughly bad mood. He found Priscilla in a corner of the lounge, poring over a book, a small frown marring her smooth forehead.

'Studying?' asked Hamish.

'I'm studying *Macbeth*. I have somehow, I don't know why, allowed myself to be persuaded into taking the role of Lady Macbeth.'

'But Angela was going to do that!'

'Harold decided she wasn't tall enough.'

'I'm surprised you should bother.'

'The village is all excited about it. It'll be good for the schoolchildren.'

'Fond of this Harold Jury, are you?'

'A very interesting and intelligent man.'

'Aw, come on!'

'Hamish, let's face it, the conversation around here can get a bit tedious. There are only four subjects – sheep, fishing, the weather, and more sheep.'

'And murder,' snapped Hamish, turning and stalking off.

Hamish decided to go back to the castle. He wanted to look in Irena's room again. If she had been blackmailing someone and it had something to do with the family, she might have hidden something somewhere. It was a faint hope because he had checked the room thoroughly – and the forensic team would then have gone over it.

There were no press waiting outside the gate. He stopped and spoke to the policeman on guard. 'Still busy up at the castle?'

'No, they've all gone back to Strathbane. The family's still here.'

'What about the Russian?'

'Herself's gone back to Lochdubh.'

Hamish drove on. No attempt had been made to put anything in the way of a garden in front of the castle. The locals must have been allowed to graze their sheep on the turf or – most likely – have just driven their sheep in when the castle was empty. The turf of what had once been a lawn was short and springy.

He was met in the hall by Andrew – short, hairy, and truculent Andrew – who glared at him. 'What now?' he demanded.

'I'll just be having a wee keek at Irena's room again.'

Andrew stared at him for a long moment and then said, 'You're that copper she was going to marry, aren't you?'

'That's right.'

'Could you do with a drink?'

'A coffee would be fine.'

'Come into the kitchen. There's still some in the pot.'

Wondering at this sudden friendliness, Hamish followed Andrew into the kitchen.

The kitchen was half modernized with gleaming fittings along one wall, but the old kitchen range still dominated the other, and the floor was stone-flagged and cold. In fact, the whole kitchen was cold.

Hamish asked for a black coffee. 'Sit down at the table,' said Andrew. 'This is a bad business.'

'I'm sure the police will soon decide they have questioned you enough,' said Hamish, 'and then you can all leave. Will you sell this place?'

'I honestly can't think anyone would want it. Why did you want to marry Irena?'

'She came to me in great distress. Mrs Gentle had fired her. She was worried about her visa and what she would do when it ran out. I know it sounds silly now, but she was so upset that I decided to marry her. That way she could stay. I don't want to distress you, but you must have heard by now that Mrs Gentle, or someone who was helping her, may have killed Irena.'

'That's ridiculous. Think of the difference in size alone. Irena was a great big strapping girl, and my mother was old and frail.'

'I don't think she was exactly frail. Irena was killed by a sharp blow to the head. Given enough time and peace and quiet, your mother could well have dragged her over and tipped her into the trunk.'

'I still can't believe it. Did Irena confide in you much?' asked Andrew.

'No. It stands to reason,' said Hamish. 'I thought I was helping a Turkish girl called Ayesha, not a top-flight Russian hooker.'

'I'll leave you to finish your coffee,' said Andrew abruptly, and rose and left the room.

Hamish stared after him. Now, there's someone worried that Irena told me something the family don't want me to know. He was suddenly hungry. There was a loaf of bread on the counter. He cut two slices, then opened the fridge, took out a packet of butter and one of ham, and made himself a couple of sandwiches. He poured another cup of coffee and sat down at the table.

He was interrupted by daughter Sarah. 'What do you think you are doing?' she demanded.

'Mr Andrew Gentle kindly offered me coffee and told me to take my time finishing it,' said Hamish blandly. 'I brought my sandwiches with me,' he added, hoping that Sarah would not notice the loaf was now missing two slices.

She sat down suddenly next to him and ran her fingers through her hair. 'This is awful.'

'It should be over soon.'

She clutched his arm. 'You *know*?'

'I simply meant you should be able to leave very soon. Do you think it possible that your mother could have killed Irena?'

'I confess I found my mother pretty cruel. But murder! No, it's ridiculous. She liked power over people, you know. She often wondered out loud why Irena put up with it, and wondered whether she were an illegal alien. If only my mother hadn't been murdered after Irena was killed, I might have thought Irena had done it.'

'At the family party, could Irena have possibly overheard anything that might lead her to blackmail your mother? I mean, why should Mrs Gentle, after having treated her so badly, suddenly decide to give her a wedding reception and ten thousand pounds?'

'Nothing I can think of. There was a lot of friction because Mark was stirring things up, oiling to Mother and being poisonous to all of us behind her back.'

'He must be delighted that he benefits from the will and Mrs Gentle didn't have time to change it.'

'He should be the prime suspect, but it appears he has a cast-iron alibi.'

'Do you all have alibis?'

'Yes, of course. But the police seem determined to try to break them. That's why we're still all here. That Russian inspector is the worst. She raps out question after question.'

John Gentle, Sarah's nephew, drifted into the kitchen. 'Consorting with the enemy, Sarah?'

'I think he's on our side,' said Sarah with a measured look at Hamish. 'After all, Irena nearly tricked him into marriage.'

John smiled maliciously as he settled himself into a chair opposite Hamish. 'She was trying to hook a bigger fish,' he said.

'What? Who?' demanded Hamish.

'Our dear Mark, that's who. She was flirting with him like mad. They went out for a walk together. When they came back, I heard them in the hall. Irena was crying quite prettily and saying, "You must help me. I don't want to marry this policeman." She must have overheard Mark goading us by saying he was going to inherit. You should have seen his face when Grandmother told us she was going to change her will and cut Mark out. Irena was hovering in the background. She wouldn't even look at Mark after that.'

'What is Mark's alibi again?' asked Hamish.

'Why, that he was working in Peckham in that garage of his, and his two mechanics will swear to it.'

He could have made them swear to it with the threat of losing their jobs, thought Hamish.

He rose to his feet. 'I'm just going to have another look at Irena's room.'

'Help yourself,' said John laconically.

Once in Irena's room, Hamish stood in the middle of it and looked around, trying to see if there was any hiding place he might have missed. Then he thought that if Irena had some incriminating evidence, she might not hide it in her room – which could be searched. The room was at the top of the tower, but there must be plenty of empty rooms where the servants had once slept. He went out and down the stone steps to the floor below and began to push open doors. What had obviously been the servants' rooms and a nursery were now filled with furniture which had probably been in the castle when Mrs Gentle had bought it;

she must have put it in these rooms for storage. In the old nursery, he saw a dusty bottle of beer and a glass sitting on a table by the window. The room had a fireplace which had not been blocked off. Beside the fireplace was a scuttle full of peat. He bent down and studied the grate. He was sure it had been used, and possibly recently. Perhaps Irena had come here to keep warm.

He began to search in the cupboards, taking out old toys and children's books and setting them aside. If Irena had found anything incriminating, it might have been in the form of a letter. He sat down on the floor and began to shake out all the books. Nothing.

He turned his attention to the toys: jigsaw puzzles, Monopoly, stuffed toys, and a complete Hornby train set in its original boxes. He opened up the boxes and began to lift out the engine and carriages bit by bit. He wondered as he searched if Mrs Gentle had known just how valuable a set like this was. He opened the door of the guard's van. Something gleamed black. He inserted his fingers and pulled it out. It was a miniature tape recorder.

He sat cross-legged on the floor and switched it on. Irena's voice: 'But it is dreadful that she should cut you out of her will.' And then Mark's voice, loud and clear: 'I'll kill that old bitch. She's doing it out of sheer spite.

Well, I'll spite her. She'll be dead as a doornail before she changes that will.'

Irena again: 'But you would not do anything silly, my darling?'

Mark: 'Just you wait and see! Shut up. Someone's coming.'

Then there was nothing but a long hiss. Hamish switched it off, pulled out his phone, and called Jimmy. 'You'd better get up to the castle right away,' he said, then described what he had found. He finished by saying, 'Ask to be shown up to the old nursery.'

Not only Jimmy arrived but also his sidekick, Andy MacNab, Superintendent Daviot, and Anna.

'You'd better stay in the doorway in case you want this room searched further,' said Hamish. 'Listen to this. I found it in the guard's van of the toy train.' He switched it on.

'Got him!' cried Jimmy. 'Those mechanics of his are from Eastern Europe. He probably told them they would lose their jobs if they didn't back him up. Let's go pick him up. Come along, Hamish. We'll seal off this room for now.'

Hamish stood for a long moment. He looked lost in a daze. Then he shook himself like a dog and followed them downstairs while policemen sealed the door of the nursery.

Outside the castle, he paused again as Mark was being dragged to a police car, protesting his innocence.

'That was good work,' said Daviot. 'Would you like to come with us to Strathbane?'

Hamish saw Anna sitting in the leading car.

'I'll just be off to my station,' he said mildly. 'I've been neglecting my other chores.'

A mist was descending as he drove to Lochdubh, and when he arrived at the police station Elspeth emerged from the swirling fog. 'Get ower to Strathbane,' said Hamish. 'They've arrested someone. I'm not authorized to tell you anything more.'

Elspeth fled into the mist. Hamish went inside to a welcome from his pets. He lit the stove and made himself a cup of coffee, then sat down at the table and began to worry. Mark's voice on the tape had not actually confessed to the murder. Certainly it sounded like intention to murder. But then Mark must have been in a foul temper at the news he was to be cut out of the will. People threatened to kill in the heat of the moment. Still, if he had been lying about his alibi and that was proved, then it would seem to clinch the matter.

What about that female in the phone box? Did Mark have an accomplice? Kylie Gentle was tall and thin.

He decided to go to the Tommel Castle Hotel and talk it over with Priscilla. Her cool common sense usually put things in proportion.

He took his cat and dog and left them in the hotel kitchen, where he knew they would be pampered and fed.

Mr Johnson told him that Priscilla was in the lounge with Harold Jury. Hamish strode in and without preamble said, 'I would like a word with you, Priscilla.'

'Do you mind?' demanded Harold. 'We were just going through her part.'

'I need a break,' said Priscilla, getting to her feet. 'I'll get back to it later.'

'If you go on like this,' said Harold, 'I'll need to find someone else for Lady Macbeth.'

'Do that very thing,' said Priscilla coldly.

'I didn't mean . . .' Harold began to babble, but Priscilla was already walking off with Hamish.

'Can we go somewhere quiet?' asked Hamish.

'I still have my sitting room. My parents always keep my rooms in the hope I'll come back.'

'And will you?'

'It's all right for a bit and then I just want to get to London again.'

Why? wondered Hamish. Who's there to pull you back?

But he said nothing, only following her into her small, pleasant sitting room.

'I suppose you want coffee,' said Priscilla.

'That would be grand. And maybe a sandwich?'

She picked up the phone and gave the order. 'Now,' she asked, 'what's all this about?'

Priscilla was wearing a blue cashmere sweater over a blue cashmere skirt. Her hair was as smooth and golden as ever. Hamish wondered whether she had started to tint it and hoped she had. He felt he would feel more comfortable with a slightly flawed Priscilla.

He told her what had happened, only breaking off when the coffee and sandwiches arrived, and then continuing on.

'So what is troubling you?' asked Priscilla.

'First, the woman in the phone box. Mark is not tall and slim. Second, he may have said all that in the heat of the moment. People do, you know. If his alibi is broken, then they will definitely charge him with murder.'

'What you are trying to say,' said Priscilla, as Hamish reached out the long arm of the law for another sandwich, 'is that it doesn't feel right. You think that if Mark had really committed the murder, then you would feel relief.'

'That's it,' said Hamish eagerly. 'I think that if it's not him, then we'll still have a murderer on the loose.'

'If Irena taped that bit of conversation and

146

tried to blackmail Mark, then it looks as if Mark might have killed Irena. There might be two murderers. And why just that little bit of tape? She must have had something on Mrs Gentle to make her pay for the reception and ten thousand pounds as well.'

'There was no wedding car to take her to Inverness, and none ordered,' said Hamish.

'So,' said Priscilla, 'if Irena taped that little bit from Mark, doesn't it stand to reason she might have had something on Mrs Gentle?'

'Probably. But then, once Mrs Gentle paid up, she would get the evidence back.'

'Maybe not.'

'Why?'

'It's not like a blackmailer to let whoever it was she or he was blackmailing off the hook. Hamish, what on earth came over you? It's not like you to be so taken in.'

'She was beautiful and genuinely seemed to be in distress,' said Hamish. 'I thought I was doing a good thing. I thought, here I am still unmarried. She said she was a lesbian.'

'Oh, Hamish!'

'I planned to marry her and then we'd get a divorce later. I suppose she wasn't even a lesbian. She could have been lying about that. But the real reason was that I knew if I told Daviot I was to be married, he would let me keep my police station. That really was what blinded me to her.'

'Lochdubh is all very well,' said Priscilla. 'But it can get very claustrophobic in the winter.'

'Lochdubh has everything a body could want,' said Hamish defensively.

'Ah, well, that's the difference between us.'

'I wish . . .' began Hamish, and then hurriedly crammed another sandwich in his mouth.

Priscilla waited until he had finished eating. 'Wish what?'

'Oh, that? I wish I could figure a way to get back into that nursery for another search.'

'You'll think of something.'

'Are you going back to rehearse with Harold?'

'I'll leave it. He's got a rehearsal in the village hall tonight, and I'll go to that. It's quite fun, really.'

Hamish collected his pets and went back to the police station through the ever-thickening mist.

He did a few chores around his croft, returned to the police station, and checked for messages. There were none.

He was just sitting having a cup of tea and wondering how soon he could get back into that nursery when the phone rang. It was Jimmy. He was exultant. 'We've got the bastard!' he said. 'His employees cracked and said they'd been paid to say he was there all the time. He was actually away for the time covering everything from the family reunion to the death of Irena and the murder of Mrs Gentle.'

'And does he confess to murdering Mrs Gentle?'

'Not a bit of it. We finally let him get a lawyer.'

'Jimmy, are you really sure he did it?'

'Oh, don't start, Hamish. We've got our man.'

When he had rung off, Hamish sat, thinking hard. He knew why he had proposed to Irena, but other people might think that they had been close, and that she'd perhaps confided something dangerous to him. If he spread that around, the murderer might come after him! But he would need to find a good excuse for sitting on any supposed evidence this long.

He decided to go to that rehearsal and spread the word that he did not think Mark Gentle was the killer – and something Irena had told him had made him suddenly realize it.

Chapter Eight

Let's briefly put on manly readiness,
And meet i' the hall together.
— William Shakespeare

Although he was glad that Anna had not called
on him or even contacted him, Hamish, as he
walked along to the village hall, was surprised
that Jimmy had not rung to give him further
news of Mark Gentle. He had tried to phone the
inspector but his mobile was switched off and
headquarters said he was busy.

The mist was still thick and the lights along
the waterfront shone dimly, as if suspended in
the air without any means of support.

From the loch, he could hear the gentle plash
of the waves and the far-off chug-chug of a
donkey engine. And yet he could not get the
relaxed feeling he usually had when a case
was over.

He decided to go ahead with what he had
planned and to put it around the gathering

tonight that Irena had told him something important. He knew the news would spread like wildfire all the way to Braikie.

The three witches were in rehearsal. 'A drum, a drum! Macbeth doth come,' howled Mrs Wellington as Hamish walked into the hall. A roar of laughter ensued.

'That's enough!' cried Harold. 'We'll take a break.'

There was a surge towards tables set at the side of the hall which were laden with cakes and sandwiches, a tea urn and cups.

Priscilla came to join him. 'This is great fun,' she said. 'Everyone's having a grand time although I gather there's an arrest and Banquo, that's Matthew, is over in Strathbane.'

'How do they get Jessie to say her lines without repeating the last words?' asked Hamish.

'Harold decided to ignore it. He's very patient.'

Hamish raised his eyebrows in surprise. He would have thought Harold too arrogant to be patient about anything.

'I'm still not happy about this arrest,' said Hamish.

'Not happy about the arrest?' boomed Mrs Wellington, who had overheard him.

'It's because of something Irena told me.'

'Then you should tell your superior officers.'

'I'll keep it to myself for a bit.'

'Did you hear that?' Nessie Currie asked her

sister. 'Thon Russian tart told Hamish something. I heard him telling Priscilla that he wasn't happy about the arrest.'

They bustled off to spread the gossip.

When the break was over, Hamish collected more sandwiches and tea and retreated to a table at the back of the hall to watch as the rehearsal resumed.

They were all very amateur, including Priscilla, who delivered Lady Macbeth's lines without passion but with a sort of icy disdain which was quite effective. And together it somehow worked. The mist had drifted into the hall, creating the right atmosphere for a Shakespearean tragedy.

When he went back to the police station, he could feel a light damp breeze beginning to fan his cheek. The dog and cat were out. They came and went by the large, expensive cat flap, a present from a grateful inspector Hamish had worked with on his last case. He knew they were perfectly capable of looking after themselves and that he should no longer plague Angela with them when he was going to be away for any length of time, but he could not stop worrying about them, and felt relieved when the flap banged and the pair finally strolled in.

He was about to go to bed when Jimmy rang. 'Good news, Hamish. Blair's charged Mark Gentle with the murders of Mrs Gentle and Irena even though he'll need more evidence. Mind you, he's screaming innocence. He says he came up before the family reunion to sweet-talk the old girl and make sure he was still in her will. But I can't get out of him why he thought he needed an alibi.'

'If he gets a good defence lawyer,' said Hamish, 'he might easily get off. The evidence is only circumstantial. Was Irena blackmailing him?'

'No, because, I suppose, she died before Mrs Gentle.'

'Exactly, Jimmy. There's no real leverage there for blackmail. A lot of folk threaten to kill people when they're angry.'

'Don't rain on my parade, Hamish. We've got him. Go to sleep.'

The morning dawned sunny and balmy with only thin traces of the previous night's mist. Hamish decided to go back up to the castle. The family would be preparing to leave. He wanted to take another look in that nursery. He fed Sonsie and Lugs and forced himself not to phone Angela and ask her to look after them.

When he arrived, they were all getting into their cars. 'What is it now?' asked Andrew.

'I'm just going up to look at that nursery again.'

'We don't want to wait around for you. Here's the key. Lock up when you leave. Here's my card. Post the key to me.'

Hamish went into the castle and climbed the stairs to the nursery. He carefully removed the tape from across the door, opened it, and went in.

The room was in chaos. It looked as if it had been torn apart. Even teddy bears had been ripped open. The police had made a thorough search.

He imagined Irena sitting by the fire, trying to keep warm. She must have been terrified of going back to her old life or she would not have put up with such treatment.

There did not seem to be much point in his searching for anything now. He cleared some toys off a chair by the window and sat down to think. Why had she been carrying around that small, expensive tape recorder? What had first led her to think there might be someone worth blackmailing? Why had Mark's been the only male voice on the tape?

There was a crash from somewhere below. Hamish rose and left the room, darting for the stairs. He gained the last stretch of stairs leading to the hall, leaping down the stairs three at a time.

He searched all over. A heavy pot was lying on its side on the stone flags of the hall. That must have been the crash he had heard.

He ran outside and looked down the drive. No one was in sight.

He made his way back into the castle and began to walk slowly up the stairs. He stopped dead before he reached the first landing. A wire was stretched across the second step. If he had not been leaping down the steps but taking them one at a time, he could have tumbled down and broken his neck on the stone flags of the hall below.

He took out his phone and called Jimmy.

Jimmy listened impatiently as Hamish told him how he had set himself up as bait and about the wire on the stairs.

'I don't want to know this,' he groaned. 'But wait there. I'll be right over.'

Hamish went outside. There was a small gravelled parking area in front of the castle. It did not seem to have been disturbed.

He walked round the castle. At the side was the kitchen door. He tried it. It was locked. He examined the lock closely, but there did not seem to be any sign that someone had tried to pick it. He walked to the back. He could see where chunks of the cliff had fallen into the sea over the years, leaving the castle perilously close to the sea's edge. There was no door at the back.

He returned to the front and entered the castle again. He had finished searching the last room when he heard Jimmy arrive.

Hamish went out to meet him. 'I didn't bring anyone with me,' said Jimmy. 'I just hope it was someone in the family leaving that wire there in case of burglars.'

'Don't be daft, Jimmy. Someone dropped that great pot in the hall, someone who knew I was upstairs and knew that I would come racing down. What we need are blueprints to this place. I could see no signs that anyone had come up to the front door or had left by that way. There must be another entrance. So far, I've searched everywhere and can't find it. Might be something in the study.'

'The case was all nicely tied up,' said Jimmy.

'Confessed, did he?'

'No, he's still protesting his innocence.'

'So let's look for blueprints.'

They went into the study. 'They might be rolled up somewhere,' said Hamish.

'There's nothing in the bookshelves that I can see,' said Jimmy.

'Might be in a big bound book,' suggested Hamish. 'Like those on the bottom shelf.'

Jimmy pulled out one and opened it. 'Victorian photo album,' he said. 'Must have been quite a place in its heyday. Look at the maids and butler lined up behind the family.'

'What about that thin one underneath?'

Jimmy tugged it out, laid it on the desk, and opened it.

'Blueprints!' he cried. 'You have a look, Hamish. I'm fair lousy at making these things out.'

'Leave me with it and go up and have a look at that wire. You'll see what I mean,' said Hamish, settling himself behind the desk.

He began to study the blueprints carefully. His eyes widened as his long finger traced a staircase. Of course! When the castle had been built, there would have been a back staircase for the servants. It led down to the kitchen. There was a small stillroom, butler's room, larder, and laundry room. The staircase led from the back of the kitchen. He called to Jimmy and when he entered the study said, 'Look at this!'

'What is it?' asked Jimmy.

'It's a staircase. The back stairs for the servants. Let's go and look.'

They made their way into the kitchen, Hamish carrying the book of blueprints, which he put on the kitchen table. He looked around. 'It should be over there where the new units have been put in.'

He knelt down and searched the floor. 'There are scratch marks here. This cupboard is on castors. Help me wheel it out.'

The cupboard slid out easily. Behind was a door. Hamish put on a pair of latex gloves and opened it. 'There are your back stairs,' he said.

'He could have come in this way. Look, there are footprints in the dust on the stairs.'

They walked up to the first landing. A door which had led off it was bricked up. On they went to the second landing. Here they found a door. Hamish pushed it open and found himself looking at the back of a large wardrobe. He edged round it and found himself in one of the bedrooms.

'That's how he did it,' said Hamish. 'He must also have a key to the kitchen door. When he heard me coming down the stairs, all he had to do was nip out the kitchen door and wait until the coast was clear. He could walk along the cliff edge and nip over the boundary wall. May have had his car parked out on the road.'

'We'd better go back downstairs and get everyone up here,' said Jimmy gloomily. 'These stairs and the kitchen have got to be dusted all over again. And I thought I was in for a few peaceful days!'

No one was pleased with Hamish Macbeth. There were grumbles at headquarters, even Daviot saying, 'Why couldn't he have left things alone, instead of setting himself up like some sort of stalking horse?'

It meant all the family had to be contacted again about the wire on the stairs, and all their alibis checked. Hours and days of police time

159

and police money. 'I've a good mind to sell that damn police station of his to recoup our losses,' raged Daviot.

The fact that they might have arrested the wrong man hung over headquarters like a black cloud.

The next morning, Hamish was in his police station when Elspeth arrived. 'I've been summoned back to Glasgow,' she said. 'Nothing to report until the court case.'

'You'd best come in,' said Hamish. 'Something's come up.'

Elspeth listened eagerly. 'This is grand, Hamish. What a story! Secret staircase and all.'

'The trouble is,' said Hamish, 'that you'll need to get the facts officially. I suggest you go up to the castle, where they're still searching for clues. I'd better give a hint to Matthew Campbell. Is he at the *Highland Times*?'

'No, he's off to cover a dried-flower show at Bonar Bridge. Don't worry. I'll fill him in when I get back. Are you going to be all right? What if the murderer tries again?'

'Don't say anything in the paper about me suggesting I really knew something, or I'll be plagued by time-wasting nutters,' said Hamish.

'I won't.'

'Now get out of here fast. I bet that Russian inspector will soon be here.'

* * *

And so it turned out. No sooner had Elspeth's car disappeared along the waterfront than Anna was at the door.

'We have to talk,' she said.

'You're in plain clothes,' said Hamish.

'I was about to leave when your news broke.' Anna was wearing a tailored grey suit over a white blouse. Her hair was tied at the back of her head with a thin black ribbon.

When she was seated at the kitchen table, she said, 'If Mark Gentle did not murder Mrs Gentle or Irena, then it might have been you.'

'How do you work that out?' demanded Hamish.

'You did not want to marry Irena, so you killed her. Mrs Gentle found out something that would incriminate you, and so you lured her out and pushed her over the cliff. You put the wire on the stair yourself so as to mislead the police.'

Hamish thought, illogically, I wish she didn't look so much like Putin in drag.

'I couldn't have killed Irena because Jimmy Anderson was with me from the early morning until we left for Inverness. Now that you all have a suspect and thought the case closed, why should I try to open it? What gave you such a crazy idea?'

'You are a man of great intelligence and yet you choose to remain in this isolated village and stay in the rank of an ordinary policeman.

Only someone who is psychologically flawed would opt for that.'

'What on earth is wrong with being contented and unambitious?' said Hamish. 'I enjoy my life here, I love this village – that is, when I am not beset by murderers and foreign police officers.'

'You forget the respect that is due to my rank!'

'It's not every day I am accused of being a murderer,' said Hamish mildly. 'Coffee?'

'Yes.'

When Hamish had served them both with coffee and shortbread, he said, 'The facts are simply these. I put it about the night before last that Irena had told me something important. I knew the gossip would spread like wildfire over the Highlands. What puzzles me about the wire across the stairs is that it is not something I would expect a cold-blooded murderer to do.'

'Why? Can't you make decent coffee? This is dreadful.'

'It's special instant,' said Hamish huffily. 'Mr Patel said it was pure Kenyan. I think the wire across the stairs is something you see in television movies. I wonder if the members of the Gentle family have all left the area. No, I think the real murderer of Irena will find something more sophisticated to do to me.'

'Aren't you frightened?' Anna took a silver flask out of her handbag and poured a shot of vodka into her coffee.

'Yes.'

'So why do it?'

'Because somehow I do not believe that Mark Gentle is a murderer,' said Hamish impatiently. 'I would be more frightened in a way if I thought a murderer had got away with this.'

'Why?'

'Do you have any children, Inspector? You know how they go on? Why, why, why, and never listen to the answer. I love this place, and it stands to reason I don't want a killer on my patch.'

'I think you're wrong,' said Anna, 'and I've got to get back to London. Let us have sex.'

Hamish coloured up to the roots of his fiery hair.

'Why?'

'Now it's you with your whys. Because it's fun and I would like sex.'

'Can't.' Hamish shuffled his boots miserably.

'Why?'

'The sheets arenae clean.' The real response, the truthful response, thought Hamish, was that he did not feel like romping with someone who looked like the Russian president.

'Are you a virgin?'

163

'No. Look, I am verra flattered that such an attractive lady as yourself should want to go to bed with me –'

'Who said anything about bed? You have a kitchen table.'

'Oh, michty me!' howled Hamish. 'It's too early in the day.'

There was a knock at the kitchen door, and Hamish leapt to answer it. Archie Maclean stood there. 'Grand news, Hamish. I'm a soldier.'

'Have you given up the fishing?'

'Och, no. In the play.'

'Come ben, Archie. This is Inspector Krokovsky. She was chust leaving.'

Anna smiled wryly and gathered up her belongings. 'If you are ever in Russia –'

'Yes, yes,' gabbled Hamish. 'I'll look you up.'

'You look as red as your hair,' said Archie. 'That wumman been givin' ye a bollocking?'

'Something like that,' said Hamish. 'Sit down. Coffee?'

'I'd like a glass of wine.'

'What on earth is this? Drinking in the morning, and wine, too.'

'I've been up all the night as you ken very well. This is the evening fur me. Besides, I'm an actor now, and them actors drink wine.'

Hamish might have sent the fisherman pack-

164

ing if he had not been afraid of Anna coming back. 'I've a bottle out in the shed,' he said. 'Someone gave it to me last Christmas.'

He went out and came back with a bottle of Merlot, which he opened. He poured Archie a glass.

Archie sipped it cautiously and made a face. 'It's gone off. Right sour taste.' He saw the sugar bowl on the table, spooned sugar into his glass, and stirred it briskly before taking another sip. 'Now, that's better,' he said.

'Did you hear folk talking lately,' asked Hamish, 'about me thinking they had arrested the wrong man?'

'Aye,' said Archie. 'Bella Firth, her what lives up the back, big blowsy wumman, she says it's because you did it yoursel' but your conscience is troubling you and you want to clear it afore you die of AIDS.'

'To think I have just been defending this place to thon Russian,' marvelled Hamish. 'Was everyone else so stupid?'

'Na. Priscilla, she said very loudly that you were never wrong and what you probably meant was that the police had made a wrong arrest and you had a good idea who the real murderer was.'

'So we'll wait and see,' said Hamish.

'Whit?'

'Nothing,' said Hamish. 'Nothing at all.'

* * *

After Archie had left, he called Jimmy on his mobile. 'Anything useful?' he asked. 'Any fingerprints?'

'No, but footprints. It was a woman.'

'And it was a woman in the phone box. You know, Jimmy, there's something awfy amateurish about that wire across the stairs. Rather as if someone had been watching Miss Marple on the telly and got the idea.'

'We're checking through the family's alibis. They all seem to have been on the road by the time you were in the castle. Of course, one of them could have doubled back. They all swear they didn't know about that staircase.'

'What about Mark?'

'They're hanging on to him for the moment.'

'Where's Blair?'

'Back in the rehab in Inverness. Maybe he'll get it this time.'

'I doubt it. While they're talking about the Twelve Steps of recovery, Blair will be plotting how to escape to the nearest pub.'

'Keep your fingers crossed that the auld scunner dies. I'm in line to get his job.'

'Joined the Freemasons?'

'No, but if that's what it takes, I'll roll up my trouser leg with the best of them. Do you want to come up here?'

'I think I'll just hang around the village and get local matters up to shape. It doesn't matter if there's a double murder, sheep dip papers must be attended to.'

'I'll leave you to it.'

For the next few days, Hamish patrolled his extensive beat, calling on the elderly in the outlying croft houses, but there was no attempt on his life.

Jimmy phoned to say that they had had to release Mark Gentle. He had hired a good lawyer who pointed out that they had nothing except a fragment of his voice on a tape. The lawyer also said that Mark had sworn he had gone on to say that unfortunately he didn't have the guts to kill anyone, which was probably why Irena had saved only the one incriminating little bit.

'Did he say anything about Irena trying to blackmail him with it?' asked Hamish.

'No, he seemed hurt and puzzled. Seemed to think Irena fancied him.'

But why, wondered Hamish as he drove through the early gloaming, had Irena kept that fragment? Did she know that someone planned to kill Mrs Gentle? Had she been in league with the murderer and kept that little bit on her recorder to help him? And had she changed her mind and decided to blackmail the murderer?

And what woman could be the murderer? Kylie Gentle, her daughter, or someone else?

What about the caterers? Was there some link there to the Gentle family? Or had there been some woman who answered the description of the woman seen in the phone box staying at the hotel where they worked?

The police would have checked up on all strangers in the area, but what if there had been some seemingly respectable lady staying at a bed-and-breakfast or somewhere else?

He drove towards Braikie, determined to interview Fiona King and Alison Queen, the chefs.

Both women seemed to be very busy in the kitchen but said they would be glad to take a break and talk to him.

'There can't be many guests at this time of year,' said Hamish.

'A lot of people travel quite a distance to come here for dinner in the evenings,' said Fiona. 'But this is really what's keeping us busy.' She handed Hamish a brochure entitled, *King and Queen, Royalties of Cooking.*

'You see, we cater for people in their homes,' said Alison. 'Because of the smoking ban in Scotland, and up here they smoke like the third world, a lot of them don't want to go out to a smoke-free restaurant. So we serve them dinner in their own homes where they can smoke themselves to death in comfort.'

'I forgot to ask you last time,' said Hamish, 'but I'm trying to find a stranger who might have been staying here or in the area. She's tall with a mole on her chin. Maybe wearing a red-and-gold headscarf and dark glasses. Dressed in a tweed jacket, shooting breeches, and brogues.'

The chefs looked at each other and then shook their heads. 'Haven't seen anyone like that, not even amongst the dinner crowd,' said Fiona.

'You hadn't met any of the Gentle family before?'

Alison giggled. 'No, and we're too busy to murder anyone.'

Hamish thanked them and left, spending what remained of the day calling at every bed-and-breakfast he could think of without success.

As he wearily crawled into bed that night, he found himself almost hoping that the murderer would make an attempt on his life. Anything to give him just one clue.

Chapter Nine

The tragedy of love is indifference.
– Somerset Maugham

Hamish, in the following days, was anxious to talk over the murder cases with Priscilla. But every time he called at the hotel, it was to be told she was either out walking with Patrick Fitzpatrick, having dinner with Patrick, or rehearsing her part with Harold.

Why Patrick? he wondered. There had been nothing very interesting about the man that he could remember. He was tall and slim, ginger hair, pursed little mouth, and reddish skin. Hardly an Adonis.

He would not admit to jealousy, but thought bitterly that for auld lang syne Priscilla should at least have made herself available to act as his Watson.

He called on Angela Brodie instead. To his amazement, the usually messy and unhygienic kitchen was clean, the many cats confined to the garden.

'What happened?' he asked, looking around. 'Expecting a visit from the health inspector?'

'Don't be nasty, Hamish. I've been reading a self-help book. It says, in effect, that if you are not getting on with your work, it could be because of the mess at home, or because you are working in a dirty office. Would you like a coffee?'

'Fine.' Hamish quite often shied away from Angela's offers of coffee, expecting to find some awful cat hairs sticking to his mug, because the cats too often roamed the kitchen table, licking the butter and drinking out of the milk jug. 'It'll save you a lot of vet's fees,' he added, removing his peaked cap and sitting down. Only two weeks before, one of the cats had ended up with its head stuck firmly in the milk jug.

'It hasn't helped a bit with the writing,' said Angela. 'Instead of being compulsive about finishing this latest book, I've become compulsive about cleaning.'

A dismal yowling started up outside.

'That's it!' Angela turned to open the kitchen door. 'Poor beasties. I can't bear it any longer. I'm going to let them in.'

'Could you wait till we've had coffee?' pleaded Hamish. 'I'll need to talk to someone.'

'What about? The fact that Irena told you something mysterious?'

'I made that up, hoping our murderer might have a go at me.'

'But you got your man. I haven't been reading the newspapers. Has something else happened?'

Hamish told her about the wire across the stairs and the female footprints.

'A woman? Who on earth could that be?'

'Probably someone who's long gone. No, wait a bit. She might just still be around the area. Jimmy told me he'd put extra men on the job, going all over the place, interviewing any visitors. Where could she be staying?'

'A tent up on the hills somewhere?'

'That's an idea. I'd better get off and tour around again.'

Angela put a mug of coffee down in front of him. 'Have your coffee first. What's happened to that Russian policewoman?'

'Gone back to London, thank goodness. She fair gave me the creeps.'

'Have you seen much of Priscilla?'

'I have not,' said Hamish huffily. 'Herself is either walking the hills with an Irishman who's staying at the hotel or rehearsing her part with Harold Jury.'

'I might call on Harold Jury again,' said Angela. 'I only met him briefly when he suggested I might like to play Lady Macbeth. It

173

would be nice to discuss writing with another author.'

'He's an odd character,' said Hamish. 'I put him down as dead arrogant and yet when I went to one of the rehearsals, I must say I was surprised at his patience.'

'Have you read his latest book?'

'No. Any good?'

'I found it a bit dull but maybe that's just me. I like stories, and that stream-of-consciousness business bores the pants off me. I'll lend it to you.'

'Can't be bothered. Well, I'm off.'

Hamish hovered in the doorway wondering whether to dare ask her to look after the dog and cat, but then decided that if he was simply going to search around the moorland and the foothills, he could take them with him.

The balmy weather had ceased, and Sutherland was gearing itself up for the long northern winter. Hamish hurried back to the police station, knowing he had better set off quickly – the sun went down at four in the afternoon.

Once the animals were put in the Land Rover along with lunch packed for all of them, Hamish drove up into the hills and along heathery little-used tracks, stopping occasionally at outlying crofts to ask if they had seen any campers.

He stopped for a picnic lunch. After his pets had been fed, he put them in the Land Rover and decided to roam across the moorland on foot before the light faded.

But all was peaceful and quiet apart from the sad piping of the curlews. Soon the shadow of the mountains fell over the landscape. He returned to the Land Rover, got in, and stared out at the fading countryside. His ruse was not working. There had been no more attempts on his life.

Back to Lochdubh, where a letter was lying on the doormat. He walked in, sat down, and opened it. It was from Elspeth. 'This is just to say goodbye,' she had written. 'Let me know if anything happens. I've been called back but can come straight back up again if you've got any news. Elspeth.'

He looked at it sadly. No 'Love, Elspeth,' not even 'Best wishes, Elspeth.'

Did he really want to marry her now? And why did he nurse that odd hankering for Priscilla? Why did he keep hoping that one day she would thaw out and become as passionate as the woman of his dreams?

The kitchen door opened and the fisherman Archie walked in. 'We was coming back this morning, Hamish,' he said, 'and I got a good look at thon folly from the sea. There's a big chunk o' the cliff has fallen and it's perched there like a toy castle balancing on someone's outstretched hand. It's now only got the lip o' the cliff to support it.'

'I'll phone up Andrew Gentle and warn him,' said Hamish. 'Sit down, Archie. Want some of that wine?'

'Na. I don't know how thae actors survive on that bitter stuff. I thocht yours had gone off but they had some at the rehearsal and it was like drinking acid. I'll take a dram.'

Hamish poured him a measure of whisky and then, after some hesitation, poured one for himself.

'You know what puzzles me, Archie?' said Hamish. 'Everyone up here knows everyone else's business. All I want to know is if someone's seen a tall strange woman about, and no one's seen anything at all.'

'Gamekeeper Geordie saw Priscilla and thon Irishman having a picnic,' said Archie. 'You chust going tae stand by and let that happen? They was up by the Beithe Burn.'

'Archie, Priscilla can do what she likes.'

When Archie had left, Hamish found Andrew Gentle's card and phoned to warn him about the perilous condition of the castle.

'There's nothing I can do about it,' said Andrew testily. 'I am sure if the damn thing falls into the sea, the insurance company will put it down to an act of God. I'll come up in the spring, hire an architect, and see if anything can be done.'

It was only when he had rung off that Hamish realized he still had the key.

He could not settle down for the evening. He felt restless. He wanted to banish Priscilla's bright image from a corner of his brain. He decided to take a run down to Inverness. It was late-night shopping, and if he hurried he could be there in time. He needed some new casual clothes.

He took Sonsie and Lugs with him. There were plenty of shops in Strathbane, the nearer town, but he wanted to get well away from Lochdubh.

But by the time he had battled round the crowded shops and bought new shirts and trousers, he was longing to get back to the peace of home. He bought kebabs for himself, the dog, and the cat, and fed them in the quiet street by the river where he had parked before setting out for home.

He decided to take the old way over the Struie Pass and whistled cheerfully as he zigzagged round the hairpin bends into Sutherland. He had just reached the famous viewpoint when the engine coughed and died. The petrol light was flashing empty. Hamish stared at it, puzzled. He had filled the tank just before arriving in Inverness. He got out with his torch, searched under the vehicle, and then shone the torch back along the road. There was no sign of any petrol leakage.

He opened up the petrol cap and put a dipstick in. The stick came out dry. He took a four-gallon tank of petrol out of the back of the Land Rover and poured it into the tank.

Still puzzled, he drove on. At the police station, he lifted his pets down from the vehicle, took the key down from the gutter, opened the kitchen door, and switched on the light.

'I don't think you pair need anything more to eat tonight,' said Hamish. 'Off to bed.'

He decided to have a cup of coffee. Coffee never stopped him from sleeping.

Hamish was about to open the fridge door when he glanced down at the floor. Soot from the stove had covered a little bit of the floor in a fine black layer, and in the middle was the faint imprint of a shoe.

He stared at it for a long moment. He guessed the wearer would take size seven shoes. That was the size of the shoe-prints on the back stairs of the castle. Size seven, British, was size nine, American – and what was that in centimetres? Did anyone in Britain know their shoe size in centimetres?

Hamish carefully lifted the lid of the stove. He had left, as usual, sticks and kindling and firelighter. What he usually did was just toss a match in and replace the lid.

He bent down and sniffed. There was a

smell of diesel. He backed off and whistled to his pets. 'Going for a walk,' he said, 'and fast.'

He hurried along to the Italian restaurant, where Willie was wiping the tables for the night. Hamish rapped on the door. 'We're closed,' said Willie.

'It's urgent,' said Hamish. 'I need to phone headquarters. There's a bomb in the police station.'

'Come in,' said Willie. 'Michty me!'

Hamish took out his mobile phone. 'Willie, start evacuating the houses around the police station. Do it quick.'

Willie ran off. Hamish got a sleepy Jimmy on his mobile number.

'Jimmy, get the bomb squad. I think someone's put a fertilizer bomb in the stove in my kitchen. I'm in the Italian restaurant. Willie Lamont's gone to evacuate the houses nearby. I'm off to help him.'

'Be with you fast,' said Jimmy and rang off.

The night was frosty so Willie ushered several families into the restaurant. Mrs Wellington, who had been telephoned for help, had taken the rest of those considered to be in the danger area up to the manse.

Hamish fretted and waited, only relaxing when he heard the sound of the sirens coming over the hills towards Lochdubh.

He walked along to the police station to meet Jimmy, who was standing there with an army bomb disposal unit.

'Tell the sergeant here about it,' said Jimmy.

Hamish described the footprint on the sooty floor and the smell of diesel.

'Any wires?' asked the sergeant.

'No. I looked.'

Two of his men went inside the police station. Hamish turned to Jimmy. 'It was the same size as the footprint we saw in the castle.'

'Damn and blast it!' said Jimmy. 'If this murderer thinks you know something, doesn't he think it odd you'd keep it to yourself?'

'He may think Irena told me something that I haven't yet figured out,' said Hamish.

The men came out, carrying something in a plastic forensic bag.

'Here it is,' said one. 'A fertilizer bomb. Nice little homemade thing. All you need is newspaper, chemical fertilizer, cotton, diesel, and you've got your bomb. Someone put the fertilizer wrapped in newspaper at the bottom of your stove, then put cotton soaked with diesel on the top. If you'd lit your stove, it would have blown apart five hundred square metres – which would have dealt with you and your police station.'

'Hamish,' said Jimmy, 'maybe we're being sidetracked by the whole Gentle family. You don't think there might be some Russian connection?'

'No, I don't. They would have caught up with her before this.'

'Maybe not. Who'd think of looking for her in the north of Scotland?'

'We should be looking for someone fairly tall and slim with size seven feet,' said Hamish. 'Might be a good idea to check Kylie Gentle's alibi.'

People were returning to their houses. The forensic team arrived and went into the kitchen.

'I'm going to go up to the hotel and see if I can mooch a room,' said Hamish. 'Oh, there's another thing, Jimmy. I was coming back over the Struie Pass when I ran out of petrol. Now, I filled the tank up just before I got to Inverness. Say someone followed me down and drained most of the tank to immobilize me so that they could race back to the station and plant the bomb?'

'Might get something on CCTV,' said Jimmy. 'Where were you parked?'

'Away down on a side street off the Ness Bank.'

'It's a pity you were too cheap to pay for proper parking. You'd best leave the Land Rover and let the forensic boys look over it.'

'Could one of your lads give me a lift to the hotel?'

'Aileen will do that. Wait a minute.'

Jimmy went off and came back with a policewoman. 'This is Aileen Drummond.'

Aileen was small and chubby with a cheeky face. When he got into the police car, Hamish said awkwardly, 'I wonder whether you might stop at that Italian restaurant on the waterfront to pick up my dog and cat?'

'No trouble,' said Aileen.

But she flinched as Sonsie and Lugs were ushered into the backseat. 'No,' said Hamish, before she could speak, 'it's not a wild cat.'

'Looks fair savage to me,' said Aileen.

'Are you from Glasgow?'

'Yes. Recognize the accent did you?'

'It's not as thick as Blair's, but yes. What's brought you up here?'

'I wanted to work in the Highlands but I landed in Strathbane, which is a sort o' Glasgow in miniature but without the culture, without the restaurants, and without the posh shops. One great heaving underclass o' criminals. You all right? Must be a hell o' a shock finding a bomb in your kitchen.'

'I'm fine.'

'Here's the hotel. Want to go in and get blootered? I could say you were in shock and needed tender loving care.'

'I don't want to get drunk, and you're driving.'

'Suit yourself.'

'Tell you what,' said Hamish, 'I'll stand you one drink.'

'You're on.'

When Hamish went into the bar, he found Priscilla with Patrick and Harold Jury, sitting at a corner table and enjoying after-dinner coffees and brandies.

Priscilla rose and came to join him. 'I heard about the bomb,' she said. 'How are you?'

'Not bad, but I need a room for the night.'

Priscilla smiled. 'Meaning a free room. I'll get you one.'

Hamish introduced Aileen. When Priscilla went off to find a room for him, Hamish asked Aileen what she would like to drink. To his relief she ordered whisky and water. The few young women he had entertained often asked for peculiar mixtures or cocktails he had never heard of.

Elspeth struggled awake later that night. Her phone was ringing. It was the night desk. 'You're to get back up to the Highlands, fast,' said the night news editor. 'That policeman was nearly blown up tonight. Someone put a bomb in his station.'

'Hamish, is he all right?'

'Yes, he escaped. They haven't found anyone for those murders yet. They've had to let that Mark Gentle go. And stop taking your own photographs or there'll be trouble with the union. I know you claimed they were taken by some highland fellow called Sean McSween, but no one's ever heard of him and the picture editor's swearing you made him up. So stop by the office and pick up Billy Southey.'

Elspeth scrambled out of bed and began to dress. Billy was a new photographer. She hadn't been out on a story with him yet. She hoped he wasn't a drunk.

Hamish had managed to get rid of Aileen after one drink by promising to take her out for dinner. He had fallen asleep almost immediately only to be awakened an hour later by the phone ringing loudly beside his bed.

It was Jimmy. 'Daviot's in a fair taking,' he said. 'He wants you hidden away. He says the attempt on your life could have killed some villagers as well. You're to pack your suitcase and come to headquarters tomorrow. I'll get you an unmarked car, and you can drive it to wherever they've decided to hide you.'

'I should stick around. The only way we might catch this female is if there's another attempt,' protested Hamish.

'Sorry, laddie. Orders are orders.'

Hamish realized after he had hung up that his pets must have been out of the police station when that bomb was planted or they would have attacked the intruder and might have been killed. Perhaps it would be better to go into hiding.

The next day, Detective Chief Inspector Blair arrived at police headquarters. He had checked himself out of rehab two days before. They had protested and told him they would send a report to Superintendent Daviot.

He made his way up to Daviot's office. Secretary Helen smiled at him. She liked Blair, who occasionally bought her flowers and chocolates.

'We didn't expect to see you for a while,' said Helen.

'I'm all right now.'

'I'm afraid Mr Daviot is busy.'

'I'll wait,' said Blair. 'Any chance of a coffee?'

'Of course.'

Helen rose and went into the small kitchen next to her desk. The morning post was lying in a basket on her desk.

Keeping an eye on the kitchen, Blair riffled through it until he found an envelope with the name of the rehab on the front. He tucked it inside his jacket and retreated as Helen returned with his coffee.

'Who's in there?' asked Blair.

'Mr Anderson and Hamish Macbeth.'

'What's up?'

'Didn't you hear? Someone tried to blow up the Lochdubh police station last night. It's the second attempt on Hamish's life, so they're going to hide him away. I had to start first thing this morning, phoning estate agents to find a suitable place.'

Blair paused, his coffee cup halfway to his lips. 'Why's someone trying to bump off yon loon?'

'The murderer seems to think Hamish knows something or something like that,' said Helen. 'Really, that man is such a load of trouble.'

'Where did you find a place?' asked Blair.

'It's top secret, you know, but of course there's no harm in telling you. I found a cottage in Grianach. Ideal place. There's just one road down into it.'

'Where is it?'

'Right up in the northwest of Sutherland, near the top.'

Hamish and Jimmy came out of the superintendent's office. 'You can go in now,' said Helen.

'And how are you?' asked Daviot, looking doubtfully at Blair. 'I thought you were going to be away for a few weeks.'

'They decided I wasn't an alcoholic,' lied Blair. 'It was all a result of a dirty trick played on me by that Russian.' He described the vodka-drinking session and ended by saying,

'You must see, sir, I couldnae do anything else, with her being a visitor and all.'

'I think, however, you should go home and get some more rest,' said Daviot. 'Detective Inspector Anderson can cope with everything.'

Blair left in a foul mood. He could see the day approaching when he would be forced into early retirement and Jimmy Anderson would get his job. And he would hate to leave the force without first getting rid of Hamish Macbeth.

And then he had a brilliant idea. If some murderer was looking for Hamish Macbeth, why not help the murderer to find him?

He checked through his notebook and then headed down to the dismal tower blocks at the docks and was soon knocking on a dirty, scarred door.

'How are you, Tommy?' said Blair to the unsavoury creature who answered the door.

'I'm jist fine, so don't you go trying tae pin anything on me.'

'I want you to do something for me. I'll pay you. Or can I put it another way: If you don't do it, I'll have you back inside as soon as I can.'

'You'll pay me?'

'Right. I want you to go over to Lochdubh, go to that bar on the waterfront, and spread a wee bit o' gossip around.'

'Like what?'
'Let me in and I'll tell you.'

Hamish drove an unmarked car down into the village of Grianach. *Grianach*, he knew, was the Gaelic for 'sand', and sure enough there was a small sandy beach at the front of the tiny village. He had decided to call himself William Shore.

To the side of the beach was a jetty with a lone fishing boat bobbing at anchor. The village consisted of a few fishermen's cottages, a small church, and a general store and post office.

He went into the tiny dark shop. He wondered how it managed to survive. There was a musty smell of old grain and the scent of paraffin from a heater.

A small man appeared from the back of the shop. He was almost dwarf size, and Hamish felt an unreasonable stab of superstitious unease. For the fairies, which now only the old people believed in, were not glittery little things with wings but small, dark, troll-like men.

A half-remembered poem learned at school came into his head.

Up the rocky mountain.
Down the rushy glen.

We dare not go a-hunting
For fear of little men.

The shopkeeper had a thick thatch of black hair and bright green eyes. His face was sallow, his nose large, and his mouth very long and thin.

He asked Hamish in Gaelic what he wanted. With an effort, Hamish managed to reply in the same language, saying he was looking for Third Cottage.

The man replied that if he went out of the door, turned left, and went up the brae, the cottage was the last one on the left.

Hamish had brought groceries with him, but, to be polite, he bought a loaf of bread, two tins of baked beans, and a slab of Mull cheddar. Then he got back into his car and drove up a cobbled lane until he found the house. He unlocked the cottage door and went in.

The cottage was cold and smelled damp. There was a fireplace but no coal, peat, or logs. The living room was furnished with a scarred round table and two upright chairs. A couple of canvas director's seats of the kind sold for a few pounds in petrol station shops were placed on either side of the fire. The floor was stone-flagged with only a ratty rug to cover a little of it. The kitchen was in a lean-to at the back, along with a bathroom where the tub was browned by peaty water. The toilet had the lid missing. The kitchen boasted a battered electric stove, an electric kettle, and a small fridge; in the cupboard were a few cups and plates along with a frying pan and one pot. Then there was the 'best' room, the one traditionally kept for funerals and weddings. It had a three-piece suite in uncut moquette, badly stained, a small television set, a standard lamp, and a badly executed oil painting above the mantelpiece of hills and heather.

He moved through to the bedroom: one double bed with army-type blankets and a slippery green quilt, a large old wardrobe, and a bedside table with the King James Bible on it.

He sighed and went back to the car and let the dog and cat out. He carried in a box of groceries and then his suitcase and fishing rod and tackle.

He was just putting down bowls of water in the kitchen for the animals – glad he had brought bowls along, for there were none in the kitchen – when there came a knock at the door.

He opened it and looked down at the small, round woman who stood there. 'I've brought you some of my scones,' she said. 'I'm Ellie Mackay from ower the road.'

'That's verra kind of you. Come ben,' said Hamish. 'Would you like some tea?'

'No, I've got to get on.' She had a cheerfully rosy face and grey hair showing from under a headscarf.

'Do you know where I can get some peats or coal?' asked Hamish.

'There's a wee shed in the back garden,' she said. 'There wass stuff in there. This wass supposed to be a holiday let but the holiday folk last time round took wan look at the place and cleared off.'

'I'm right surprised you get any visitors at all.'

'Oh, we get a busload every second week.'

'Tourists?'

'Aye, it's a firm what calls itself Discover Secret Scotland.'

'Surely they pack up after the summer. There's hardly any light up here now.'

'They come round the midday. A blessing it is, too. There are a few folks here that carve wooden things – you know, little statues, candlesticks, things like that. Callum down at the stores sells them. He only speaks the Gaelic to them because they love that. But when the bus arrives, we've got stalls out on the harbour.'

'Where's the best place to fish?'

'If you go on up the road a bit, you'll come to the Corrie River. You don't need a permit and if you're lucky, you might be getting a few trout.'

* * *

After she had gone, Hamish went out to the shed in the garden and found slabs of peat stacked up, a sack of coal, a pile of logs, and some kindling. He was amazed the locals hadn't raided it.

He decided to go fishing while it was still light and set off for the river with his rod, the dog and cat following behind. He fished contentedly, catching four trout before the sky turned pale green, heralding the long, dark winter night.

The bus was a problem, but no one knew where he was, so he had nothing to fear. Back at the cottage, he lit the fire in the 'best' room, glad that it seemed to be drawing well, and then went through to the kitchen. He gave Sonsie a trout and fried up some deer liver he had brought with him for Lugs. Then he dipped two trout in oatmeal and fried them for his supper along with boiled potatoes and peas.

After dinner, he lay on the sofa after throwing a travel rug over it, and settled down to read an American detective story. Hamish liked American detective stories where the hero seemed to be always partnered with some beautiful female with green eyes and high cheekbones. He liked particularly the ones that were comfortingly familiar. The hero would at one point be suspended and then brought back with the grim warning, 'You've got twenty-four hours.' He got to the bit where the hero was beating up the villain. Good thing he's not in Britain, thought Hamish cynically, or the villain would sue for assault.

His mobile phone rang. He sat up and tugged it out of his pocket.

It was Elspeth. 'How are things in Grianach?' she asked.

Although the fire was blazing, Hamish felt suddenly cold.

'How did you know?' he asked.

Chapter Ten

In the highlands, in the country places,
Where the old plain men have rosy faces,
And the young fair maidens
Quiet eyes
                    – Robert Louis Stevenson

'Everyone in Lochdubh seems to know, Hamish. I was sent back up to cover the bomb. Shall I come and join you? Are you on holiday?'

'Is that what they are saying?'

'You know this village. Chinese whispers. But certainly that seems to be the sum total of it.'

'Elspeth, leave me alone for a bit. But you might have a story down there. I was sent up here to stop the murderer from finding me and trying again. If you can find out who was spreading the news about me, you'll at least find someone who's interested in seeing me dead. And get back to me if you've found out anything.'

'All right. Give me a few paragraphs about the bomb in the kitchen.'

Hamish gave her a brief description.

'I know Grianach,' said Elspeth. 'Weird place. They make wooden things.'

'That's right. Trouble is, a tour bus comes every two weeks.'

'And you think the murderer might travel that way to find you?'

'Perhaps. But probably too complicated.'

The next morning, Hamish went out to explore the village. It nestled at the foot of steep cliffs, and any car approaching from out-side could clearly be seen on the one-track road down into it. There was a horseshoe bay in front of the village, the waters calm in an unusually placid day. Far out beyond the bay, he could see the whitecaps of the great Atlantic waves.

He sat down on a bollard on the jetty. It was all so remote and peaceful. The air smelled of tar, fish, baking, and peat smoke.

A voice behind him said, 'Enjoying the view?'

Hamish stood up and turned round. 'I'm James Fringley,' said the man. 'I heard you've arrived.'

Racking his memory for who he was sup-posed to be, Hamish remembered suddenly that he was supposed to be Mr William Shore.

'William Shore,' he said, holding out his hand. 'You're English.'

James was a small dapper man dressed in a Barbour and jeans. Hamish judged him to be in his fifties. He had silver hair, carefully barbered, and neat features.

'Are you visiting like me?' asked Hamish.

'No, I live here. I used to be a bank manager but I took early retirement. We're about to start setting up the stalls. The bus arrives today.'

'I'm surprised a tour bus found this place.'

'I wrote to them,' said James. 'What with the fishing dying off, I thought it would be nice to help the villagers. Do you know, the European Union cut the cod and fishing quotas last December and Scotland wasn't even represented? Luxembourg was there. One tiny landlocked country having a say. It's mad. We've a lot of home industry now, and every month or so I load up the van and go south to flog the stuff around the shops. I mean, look at the beauty of this place. A man would do anything to keep it as grand as this. I'm off to the church hall to start helping with the stalls.'

'I'll come with you,' said Hamish.

'You're highland, aren't you?' asked James curiously. 'What brings a highland tourist here?'

Hamish was blessed with the highlander's facility to lie easily and convincingly. 'It was the wife,' he said. 'She threw me out. I thought if I went away for a bit, she'd come to her senses.'

'That's bad. Got children?'

'No, we've only been married three months. I blame her mother,' said Hamish bitterly. 'Awfy auld queen. What about you?'

'Mine died of cancer. We didn't have children. I came here four years ago on holiday and decided to stay. Probably the last place in Britain where you can buy a cheap house.'

The figures of the villagers could be seen approaching the church hall. 'They're all verra small,' said Hamish.

'Maybe inbreeding, but they're all sane enough.'

Hamish helped to carry trestle tables down to the harbour. Then the villagers started to set out their wares. Hamish was amazed at the wood carvings. They were very good indeed. One stall had beautiful lengths of tweed. 'That's your neighbour, Ellie,' said James. 'She's got a loom in a shed in her garden.'

Hamish decided to buy presents before the bus arrived. He bought a wooden salad bowl for his mother, two carved candlesticks for Angela, and an attenuated wood sculpture of a woman for Priscilla.

The prices were remarkably reasonable. Then he noticed a carving of a man, a fat bloated man whose face was set in a horrible sneer. It looked remarkably like Blair. Hamish bought it as a present for Jimmy.

Then he thought how much his mother

would like some tweed and bought a length of a heathery blue-and-pink mixture.

He carried all his purchases back to his cottage and returned just in time to see the tour bus make its precipitous descent of the cliff road. He walked behind a shed at the end of the harbour and looked around. The bus was full – full of elderly ladies and two elderly men.

He came out of hiding and walked towards it. Two were being helped into wheelchairs. Some walked with sticks.

Hamish went up to the tour guide, a slim woman in a yellow suit. 'Where are this lot from?' he asked.

'A retirement home in Perth,' she said. 'Great for us. They booked the whole bus, and this is a quiet time of year. I'd better go and help them with their purchases.'

Hamish was pleased to see that sales were brisk.

After half an hour of buying, the tour operator called out, 'If you will make your way to the village hall, there is a buffet lunch.'

Hamish thought a free meal was just what he needed after having spent so much, but when he got to the hall, James was at the door. 'Six pounds for the lunch, and cheap at the price.' Hamish paid up.

He collected a plate of cold chicken and salad from the buffet and sat down next to one of the elderly gentlemen who turned out to be stone deaf, so Hamish contented himself by studying the women just in case one of them might look like someone in disguise. But for a start, not one of them was tall enough to fit the description of the woman who had made that phone call.

Superintendent Daviot was told that a Miss Elspeth Grant of the *Bugle* was waiting to speak to him.

He hesitated. But he was wearing a new suit and thought he looked very fine. 'Does she have a photographer with her?' he asked.

'Yes, a sour-faced Glasgow type,' said the sergeant at the front desk.

'Send them up,' said Daviot.

He brushed back his silver hair and asked Helen to prepare coffee and biscuits. He had met Elspeth before but not the photographer, who was a sullen, middle-aged man with a bloated face.

'Do sit down, Miss Grant,' purred Daviot. 'We have met before.'

Elspeth indicated the photographer, who was crouched on the floor, taking cameras out of his box. 'That's Billy Southey.'

Helen came in with a laden tray. Elspeth waited until coffee had been poured and Helen had left before saying, 'I hear Hamish Macbeth is hiding out in Grianach.'

Daviot looked at her in shock. 'Who told you that?'

'It's all over Lochdubh, and I want to know why. Some man turned up at that bar on the waterfront and started shooting his mouth off. The thing is, if it was supposed to be such a secret, how did it leak out?'

'I will look into it right away. I do not want you to write anything just now. It is a matter of PC Macbeth's security.' He pressed a buzzer on his desk. When Helen entered, he ordered her to get Jimmy Anderson up immediately.

Blair was lurking around the detectives' room. He was waiting to see Daviot to explain he was ready to return to work. He hated the idea of Jimmy being in charge.

A policewoman appeared and called to Jimmy, 'You're to go up to the super's office right away, sir.'

'Now what,' grumbled Jimmy, heading for the door.

In Daviot's office, Elspeth was saying, 'He was a thin, scruffy man in his forties. Looked like a druggie.'

'It's a pity no one got a photograph,' said Daviot.

'Oh, but they did. A photographer from the *Highland Times* was out taking pictures for the calendar. I looked through them. He's got a shot of the harbour and people on the water-front, and that looks like our man.'

She was carrying a manila envelope which she opened, pulling out a glossy photograph just as Jimmy entered the room.

Daviot outlined what had happened and said to Jimmy, 'See if you recognize the man.'

Jimmy looked at the photograph. It showed a group of people outside Patel's grocery store. He pointed to a man in the middle of the group. 'That's Tommy Shields, drug pusher and addict. I'll find him.'

Billy began to rapidly pack up his cameras as Elspeth rose to go. 'Elspeth,' said Jimmy, 'come down to the detectives' room and I'll take a statement from you.'

No photographs, thought Daviot, disappointed. The new suit would have looked grand.

Blair looked up as Jimmy came hurrying in. 'Do you know someone called Tommy Shields?'

Feeling as if he had just gone down in a very fast elevator, Blair said, 'No, what's he done?'

'Never mind,' muttered Jimmy, switching on the computer.

'I am your senior officer,' raged Blair.

'Aye, sir, but you're not supposed to be here. Find a chair, Elspeth, and I'll take your statement. On second thoughts, I'll take it later. I'd like to find this Tommy Shields first.'

Blair lumbered to his feet and headed rapidly out of police headquarters. He had to get to Tommy before they did.

He got in his car and raced down to the tower block by the docks. The lift was broken and he had to hurry up the filthy stairs, stopping on each landing to catch his breath. At last he reached Tommy's door and hammered on it.

There was no reply. Frantic with fear, he took a small cosh out of his pocket, smashed one of the glass panes on the door, and, reaching inside, turned the handle.

There was a foul smell of booze and a sweetish smell of decay. He went into the bedroom. Tommy was sprawled across a dirty bed with a needle stuck in his arm. Blair felt for a pulse and found none.

'There is a God,' muttered Detective Chief Inspector Blair, and he fled from the flat, taking the stairs two at a time. He gained the sanctuary of his car and drove off – just in time. Two police cars swept past him going towards the tower blocks.

He had worn thick gloves the whole time, except when he had felt for that pulse. Could they get a fingerprint off a dead body? They surely wouldn't be looking for one. Of course, the fact that the flat looked broken into would start them thinking about murder, but the only fingerprints they would find on that syringe would be Tommy's.

Well, that pillock Macbeth would be safe now. He wouldn't hang around Grianach waiting to be murdered.

But that was just what Hamish Macbeth proposed doing. He told an angry Jimmy Anderson that it was their only hope of catching the murderer.

'I'll see if I can get Daviot to agree to it,' said Jimmy finally, 'but we haven't got any spare men to go all the way up there on the off-chance. We found the informant.'

He told Hamish about Tommy Shields.

'That iss verra interesting,' said Hamish, the sibilance of his accent showing he was upset. 'If you've got any spare time, see if Blair ever arrested the man.'

'Do you mean to say Blair was behind this?'

'Wouldn't surprise me. I'm not saying he murdered the man, but if he got there before you and found him dead, he must ha' been verra relieved.'

'Hamish, even if I found out Blair was behind it, I doubt if Daviot would believe me. I went up to tell him about Tommy when I got back and there was a big bunch of flowers on his desk. Daviot said, "Aren't they lovely? So

204

nice of Mr Blair to remember my wife's birth-day." Look, I'll give you a day or two longer and then you'd better get out of there. Go somewhere else.'

'I'll go back to Lochdubh. I'm not going to run away any more.'

Hamish spent a pleasant day wandering around the village and chatting to the locals. When he settled down for the evening in front of the fire, he wondered if the murderer would come for him. If I were the murderer, thought Hamish, I wouldn't drive down that road into the village. Everyone would see the car. So what would I do? I'd park a bit away at the top of the road and wait till it was after midnight. The weather's on the turn, and there's no moon tonight. I'd come quietly down into the village. But how would I know which cottage?

He lay back on the sofa and stared up at the nicotine-stained ceiling. He should really report this place to the Scottish Tourist Board, he thought. What a dump for a holiday let! His eyes began to close, and soon he was fast asleep.

He was awakened by a hammering at the door and the voice of his neighbour, Ellie, shouting, 'There's a fire down by the harbour!'

He made for the door and then stopped.

That's it, he thought. Light a big fire, get every-one running out of their cottages, and wait.

'You go ahead,' said Hamish.

He pulled a black woollen cap over his head, then pulled a sweater on over his shirt. He left the cottage quietly and headed towards the river. He had seen a track leading along the side of the river up to the top of the cliffs. Near the top, he turned and looked back. A shed by the harbour had been set on fire; the locals were passing buckets of water, one to the other, to throw on the flames.

Hamish gained the road and walked along to the west, looking for a parked car. He then turned and walked back along to the east. At last he saw it on a bend of the road. It was a small battered-looking van, and the number plates had been removed.

He tried the handles at the back and found that the van was unlocked. He climbed inside, shut the doors behind him, and settled down to wait.

An hour had passed when he heard the sounds of someone approaching. Let her drive off a bit, thought Hamish grimly, and then I'll have a surprise for her.

The driver's door opened. He heard the engine roar into life, and in a split second he realized he had not heard the driver's door close.

He tore open the back door of the van, tumbled out, and leapt, seeing nothing but blackness below him. His flailing hands caught hold of a branch sticking out of the cliff. He clung on for dear life.

There was the sound of an explosion far below, and then flames shot up into the night sky.

He saw he was hidden by the overhang of the cliff. His arms felt as if they were about to be torn from their sockets. He kicked his boots into the soft ground of the cliff until he found footholds and felt the pressure on his arms slacken.

In the light from the flames below, he saw a rocky ledge to his left. With all the strength left in his arms, he swung himself over and fell panting on the ledge. Using tufts of grass for purchase, he swung himself back up over the top of the cliff and, taking out a powerful torch, swung it to the left and right.

Moorland stretched for miles either way. He pulled out his mobile phone and woke up Jimmy Anderson.

'I'll get the police helicopter up and we'll search the moors,' said Jimmy. 'Go back and lock yourself in.'

Hamish stayed awake, listening to the sound of the police helicopter overhead. At last he could not bear the inactivity any longer and went out. The harbour was full of police cars.

A forensic team was working on the burnt-out van, which had fortunately hit a large rock instead of plunging on down on to one of the houses.

James Fringley appeared beside him. 'I gather you're not who you said you were,' he said.

'No. Who told you?'

'A copper asked me which cottage had been rented to Hamish Macbeth. I gather that's you and you're that policeman from Lochdubh. Why are you here?'

'Headquarters has me hidden up here because some murderer is after me,' said Hamish wearily.

'Do me and everyone in this village a favour and get the hell out of it as soon as you can. There were fishing nets burnt in that shed, and that van could have killed someone.'

Hamish guessed the would-be killer had probably guessed he would search for him up on the clifftop. The back of the van had been cramped, and he had changed his position from time to time. Maybe the van had rocked a little, alerting the murderer to the fact that he was inside.

Jimmy arrived at Hamish's cottage at six in the morning to find the policeman still awake, packed and ready to leave.

'No success,' said Jimmy. 'We kept the heli-copter up as long as we could but then Daviot came on the phone screaming about the cost. All we can do now is put a police guard outside your station.'

'I'll alert the villagers,' said Hamish. 'Any strange woman appearing in Lochdubh and they'll make a citizens' arrest. There is no need for a police guard. Do you know, I don't think she or he will try again. I think whoever it is could possibly be mad, and made even madder with fear that I might guess something.'

'It's up to you. What a dump this place is. Worse than Lochdubh.'

'It's really lovely,' said Hamish. 'That reminds me. I've a present for you.'

He took out the wood carving that looked so like Blair.

'Man, that's grand,' said Jimmy. 'Can I stick pins in it?'

Lochdubh looked reassuringly the same. As soon as he had unpacked, Hamish got into bed, joined by his cat and dog, and fell sound asleep.

He awoke in the late afternoon to find Elspeth standing over him.

'You cannae chust walk into a man's bed-room!' he howled.

'I came to see if you were alive,' said Elspeth. 'I bought you a present.'

'I don't want a present,' said Hamish sulkily. 'All I want iss a bit o' peace.'

'Smell something?' asked Elspeth.

Hamish propped himself up on the pillows and sniffed the air. 'Coffee?'

'Yes, good coffee. I bought you a percolator.'

'Have you seen Sonsie and Lugs?'

'Last time I saw them, they were strolling along the waterfront, heading for the Italian restaurant. They must be hungry.'

Hamish got out of bed and stretched and yawned. Then he realized he had not put on any pyjamas and was stark naked.

Elspeth giggled. 'That's quite a blush you've got, Hamish. It goes all the way –'

'Get out!' he roared.

When Hamish had washed and dressed, he found Elspeth in the kitchen. She poured him a cup of coffee.

Hamish drank a little and then smiled. 'This is grand. Thank you. Now, what do I have to do for this?'

'Nothing. There's a clampdown on reporting what happened up in Grianach. Editor's phoned all over. Story suppressed. Unless you can think of anything, I've got to get back to Glasgow.'

Hamish looked at her thoughtfully. She had lit the stove. The kitchen was warm. She was wearing a chunky grey sweater over jeans, and the grey seemed to highlight the odd silvery colour of her eyes. Her hair had reverted to its usual frizzy look, which seemed to suit her better than when it was straightened.

'I may be back,' said Elspeth. 'The editor of the *Highland Times* is retiring, and Matthew is taking over as editor. He'll need a reporter.'

'Wouldn't it seem a bit tame after the city?'

'Not with the goings-on you seem to conjure up. I'm highland to the bone, and I don't really seem to fit in in Glasgow. Then the photographer I have with me, Billy, is a complete lout. All he does is sneer at this place, and the more he sneers at it, the more I realize how much I love it.'

'I was sorry to hear about you being jilted,' said Hamish. Elspeth had been left at the church on her wedding day. She had been about to marry a fellow reporter but he had run off and left her. 'Were you very hurt?'

'I was angry and then I was relieved,' said Elspeth. 'And while we're on the subject of jilted people, how are you getting on with Priscilla?'

'I cancelled the engagement,' said Hamish. 'Not her. I havenae seen much o' her. She's traipsing around the hills and heather with that Irishman.'

'Not any more. He's left, and she's too busy rehearsing her part with that writer. I'm still

211

amazed you actually got around to proposing marriage to someone, Hamish. That Russian, I mean.'

He sighed. 'I thought I was doing the right thing, Elspeth. I did it to keep my police station. And the idea was that we'd divorce after a while.'

'It's wonderful how you got permission to marry her so easily. They're clamping down on these arranged marriages. There was a woman down in England who charged a hefty fee to marry foreigners. When they caught up with her, she'd married five and not a divorce paper in sight.'

Hamish suddenly remembered the day he had bought an engagement ring to present to Elspeth, only to find out that she had promised to marry her fellow reporter.

He had bought Irena another ring. He wondered what had happened to it. Inspector Anna had arranged to have the body flown back to Moscow for burial. Why she had persuaded her bosses to go to that expense, he did not know.

He suddenly decided to take the plunge. 'Excuse me a minute,' he said. He went into the bedroom and took the ring in its little box out of his bedside table. His heart was hammering.

Just as he walked into the kitchen, the door opened and Priscilla walked in.

Hamish stuffed the box in his pocket and shouted, 'Damn it, don't you ever knock?'

'I'm off,' said Elspeth hurriedly.

'I'll come with you,' said Priscilla. 'It seems I am not welcome.'

Say something, yelled a voice in Hamish's head. But he stood there, frozen, as they both walked off.

He walked along to the Italian restaurant to be told that his animals had been fed and then had gone away.

By asking people on the waterfront, he learned that they had been spotted heading for Angela Brodie's cottage.

Angela opened the door to him. 'I've sent them home,' she said. 'The poor things seemed so hungry that I fed them first.'

'Angela, they'll be as fat as butter. They've already been stuffing themselves at the Italian restaurant.'

'Oh, well, they say that pets take after their owner, and you always were a moocher, Hamish. I suppose you want a coffee.'

'No, I do not. I haff the verra good coffee-maker. Elspeth gave it to me.'

'Did she, now. You ought to marry that lassie, Hamish.'

Hamish stared down at her, his mouth

slightly open and a vacant expression on his face.

'What's up?' asked Angela. 'You look as if you've been struck by lightning.'

'I've been struck with a flash o' the blindingly obvious,' said Hamish.

He turned and ran to the police station, got into the Land Rover, and sped off to the Tommel Castle Hotel.

He erupted into the manager's office. 'Where's Elspeth?' he asked. 'Which room?'

'Oh, she's gone. Left about ten minutes ago. Coffee?'

Hamish slumped down in a chair in the office.

'Why not?' he said.

When he left the manager's office, he stood in the reception wondering whether to chase after Elspeth. But that sudden desire to ask her to marry him had faded. He sighed. Perhaps when this case was solved – if it ever was solved – he might take a trip down to Glasgow.

'Got over your bad temper?' asked Priscilla, interrupting his thoughts.

'Sorry about that,' said Hamish. 'This case is getting to me. Murderers are usually stupid and have nearly got away with it before because they were lucky amateurs and the last people you would suspect. But this one isn't an amateur. The only amateur attempt was that wire on the stairs.'

'I've heard weird and wonderful stories about what happened up at Grianach.'

'Still no odd strange woman booked in here?'

'No, only Polish maids. Do you know the *Northern Times* has brought out a free Polish newspaper?'

'Maybe the *Highland Times* will do the same.'

'Not enough up here as yet. Have dinner with me and tell me about it.'

Hamish hesitated. Priscilla smiled. 'Sonsie and Lugs will be fine. Gosh, it's like dealing with a man with a possessive wife waiting at home.'

'All right, then. That would be grand.'

Over dinner, Hamish told her all about the happenings in Grianach. When he had finished, Priscilla said, 'You must still be in shock. Have you considered that?'

Hamish stared at her for a long moment. Was he? Was that what had prompted his sudden desire to propose to Elspeth? And it was hard to think of Elspeth with the cool beauty of Priscilla facing him across the table.

'I might be,' he said.

'I called on your mother the other day,' said Priscilla. 'I was over in Rogart and thought I would look her up. You should go home a bit more often, Hamish.'

'I'll try. I bought presents for her in Grianach. Oh, I've one for you. Ma was so upset about the wedding. She made me feel ashamed, particularly when it got out that Irena was a prostitute.'

'So what happens now?'

'I think I'll spend the next few days writing down everything I know. They might give me time off. I'm tempted to go down to London and talk to Kylie Gentle. I can't ignore the fact that it must, somehow, have something to do with that family.'

Chapter Eleven

*I think for my part that one half of
the nation is mad – and the other
half not very sound.*
             – Tobias Smollett

Hamish was granted leave. Daviot seemed
relieved that he would be out of the way.
Jimmy said that the van had been stolen from
outside a croft near Grianach. He supplied
Hamish with Kylie Gentle's address in London
but warned him that he was on his own. He
would need to cover his own expenses.

Jimmy had a further bit of astonishing news.
Blair was back on the job and sober. 'He's
found God,' said Jimmy. 'He keeps a Bible on
his desk and lectures us all on our sins. He was
a nasty bully when he was drunk and now
he's even nastier. The man's a right religious
maniac.'

'Won't last long,' said Hamish cynically.

'One setback and he'll be screaming that God doesn't exist and straight down to the pub.'

Anxious not to leave his pets too long, Hamish drove to Inverness and took an early plane to London. Kylie and her husband lived in a flat in St George's Mansions in Gloucester Road in Kensington.

He took the tube to the Gloucester Road tube station and walked along until he reached St George's Mansions. He rang the bell marked GENTLE, hoping his journey wouldn't turn out to be a waste of time with them gone on holiday somewhere. But Kylie herself answered on the intercom. When Hamish announced himself, there was a little gasp of surprise, and then he was buzzed in.

Kylie, looking like an elegant stick insect, stood in the doorway to greet him. 'What's happened now?' she asked crossly. 'The police have already been round asking if any of us have been near a place called Grianach. I told them we'd never even heard of it. Come in.'

Hamish, feeling uncomfortable in all the glory of his best suit, collar, and tie, followed her into a pleasant living room.

'It's got nothing to do with that,' he said. 'I can't help feeling that something happened at your family reunion that maybe gave Irena the idea she could blackmail someone apart from Mark.'

218

'Sit down,' said Kylie. 'Didn't we go through that all before?'

'I thought maybe you might have had time to think of something.'

Hamish studied her covertly. Could she be the murderer? Could she be trying to protect someone?

Her face was Botoxed into expressionlessness. She stared at him for a long moment. Then she said, 'It was the usual business, my mother-in-law demanding we all run around her, hinting that if she did not have the correct amount of grovel, she'd leave her money elsewhere. Mark was oiling about. Then he suddenly got furious. He'd got the news that she planned to change her will. He was talking a lot to Irena. Then he suddenly seemed to get cheerful again. Oh, he made one odd comment. He said, "There's a bastard in every family and a skeleton in every cupboard, isn't there, Auntie?" Mrs Gentle went quite white with rage.'

'I think I might pay a call on him,' said Hamish. 'Where is he?'

'I'll write it down for you. It's a garage in Peckham.'

Hamish looked up the address in a battered old copy of the London A to Z he had brought with him. He found the nearest tube station on the map and set off.

It was a cold, dusty, windy day. London seemed much dirtier than he remembered.

When he found the garage, it was closed. He asked around and was told it had been closed for the last week. No one knew where the workers were.

He pulled out his phone and asked Kylie where Mark Gentle lived, hoping it would be somewhere nearby, but Kylie gave him an address in East India Docks.

It took him an hour and a half to get there. Mark's flat was in the middle of what had been damned as Yuppie Town. Nothing but flats for the City workers. No shops or pubs or churches.

Mark lived in a small converted Victorian warehouse fronting on to one of the old docks. Hamish rang the bell, but there was no reply. He rang all the bells until a woman answered, and he said, 'Police. Let me in. I'm looking for Mark Gentle.'

She buzzed him in. He mounted the stairs to Mark's flat and hammered on the door. He could hear the sound of rap music coming from inside. He knocked again.

He took out a bunch of skeleton keys and fiddled with the lock for half an hour until he got the door open. His heart sank as he recognized the smell.

He walked in through a small hall into a large living-room-*cum*-kitchen. Mark Gentle lay sprawled on the floor. The back of his head was matted with dried blood, and there was a pool of dried blood on the floor. He still had a wineglass clutched in one hand; over by the window, a bottle lay on its side.

Rap music was belting out from a stereo. Hamish switched it off.

He pulled on a pair of latex gloves. He could do nothing for Mark now. The man looked as if he had been dead for at least a few days. He would need to call the police, but he wanted to search first.

There were two bedrooms. One had been turned into an office. The drawers in a large desk had all been pulled out, and papers were spread over the floor. He examined a computer and found that the hard drive had been taken.

Hamish knelt down and began to go through the papers but they seemed to be all to do with the garage: receipts, orders for spare parts, and wage slips.

Even the wastepaper basket had been emptied out on the floor. His eye was caught by a crumpled sheet of pink paper. He picked it up and smoothed it out. It was a letter. He glanced down at the signature. Margaret Gentle! She had written, 'Dear Mark, You can come and stay if you like, but I am going to change my will. I am leaving everything equally to Sarah and Andrew. You have only

221

yourself to blame by thinking you could blackmail me.'

So he knew about her plans to change the will before he even went there, thought Hamish. Had he decided he needed an alibi because he had something more sinister in mind than blackmail? I'll never know now, he decided. He carefully wiped the front door in case he had left any fingerprints.

He wondered what to do. If he phoned the police and waited for them, he would be in grave trouble for arriving on their territory without telling them. Strathbane would be furious. Blair would make the most of it.

The woman who had buzzed him in had not seen him. His flaming red hair was covered in a black wool cap, which he had put on when he had walked from the Docklands Light Railway station.

His footprints would be all over the place. But if he wiped the floor, he would be destroying evidence. Mark Gentle had known his killer. The bottle and glass seemed to tell Hamish that he had poured himself a drink with his back to his visitor when he had been struck down. He wished he had not called out 'Police!'

He sighed. He would have to do his duty. There was no getting away with it. He remembered seeing a surveillance camera over the door. The only lie he would tell was that he had found the door unlocked.

Hamish was grilled by the Metropolitan Police for two days, periodically being questioned when he wasn't actually being shouted at. Orders had come down from Strathbane that he was, on his return, to stay at his police station, suspended from duties, until a disciplinary hearing.

The surveillance camera over the door turned out to be empty of tape. At first it was thought that the murderer might have removed it, but it was found to be only cheapness on the part of the landlords.

Hamish did not tell anyone that Jimmy Anderson had known what he was doing, considering that one of them in deep trouble was enough.

It was at the end of Hamish's second day in London that the atmosphere suddenly thawed. It was actually said that the Met thought he had done good work and were prepared to forgive and forget. He was told that on his return, he should go back to his normal duties. There was to be no disciplinary hearing.

He was just leaving Scotland Yard when a familiar voice said, 'Hamish!'

He turned round. Anna Krokovsky stood

there, smiling at him. 'We go for dinner,' she said.

'I'm rushing off to the airport to try to catch the plane,' said Hamish.

'Nonsense. You owe me dinner after all I have been doing for you.'

'Oh, that's why ... You spoke up on my behalf.'

'Of course I did. The fools. It would have taken them ages to find that body. There is a good Italian restaurant near here.'

Hamish gave in. It was turning out to be an expensive trip. In the short time between bouts of questioning, he had had to run out and buy a clean shirt and underwear. He had been lodged in a police flat with a large boozy constable who had a vehement hatred of the Scots and said so at great length.

'Why are you still here?' he asked Anna when they were seated in the restaurant.

'I am nearly finished. I leave for Russia next week.'

'Why did you go to the trouble of having Irena's body flown home?'

'That was on the instructions of Grigori Antonov, her former protector. Strangely enough, he still seemed to retain an affection for her. Odd. He could have bought any pretty female he wanted. Now, from your investigations, it seems that Mark found out something about Mrs Gentle that she did not want known.'

'There was that "bastard in every family" remark,' said Hamish. 'Could it be that Mrs Gentle had had at one time an illegitimate child?'

'They are still searching the records.'

'The footprints in the flat were size seven,' said Hamish, 'or so they told me. That surprises me because I'm convinced our murderer is still in the north. How long had he been dead?'

'A week. But you came down, planning to be here only for the day.'

They ordered their food.

'I did not for a moment think I would find another dead body,' said Hamish. 'I was still looking for thon mysterious woman. I went to talk to Kylie Gentle again. She said something about Mark talking to Mrs Gentle about a bastard and a skeleton in the closet.'

'So you think there might be some illegitimate member of the family lurking around?'

'Maybe not. Maybe "bastard" was just a curse.'

'I feel if you dropped the whole thing – you personally – then there would be no more threats on your life.' Anna rolled a generous forkful of linguine and thrust it into her mouth. Tomato sauce rolled down her chin like blood.

'I cannae do that!' exclaimed Hamish. 'Leave a murderer on the loose?'

'Why not? Cases are unsolved every day.'

'Is this what you do in Moscow? Have three murders and chust walk away?'

'If my life was threatened, I might,' said Anna. 'You should be flattered. Our murderer obviously rates your intelligence highly.'

'I think it's because I put it about that Irena had told me something significant.'

'And do you know anything?'

'Not a thing,' said Hamish. 'You've got tomato sauce on your chin.'

'But surely the murderer would expect you to convey any knowledge to the police.'

'Not if he or she is a secretive plotting madman or woman. But it must be a woman. There are the footprints and the woman in the phone box.'

'Could be an accomplice.'

They talked on, turning over ideas, until Hamish glanced at his watch. 'If I hurry,' he said, 'I can catch the late-night flight to Inverness.'

'Go on, then. I will pay for this meal and put it on expenses.'

Hamish thanked her and fled. He did not return to the police flat, considering that he was only sacrificing some dirty laundry and a disposable razor.

When he finally arrived at the police station

in Lochdubh, it was to find a message from Jimmy telling him to send over a full report and take a few days off.

As he struggled along the waterfront the following morning, bending his lean form before a vicious gale, he decided to go to Patel's and buy some groceries.

The shop was busy, and a poster behind the counter advertised the production of *Macbeth*. It was to be shown in two days' time.

Hamish bought a ticket. 'Eight pounds!' he exclaimed.

'A lot of money was spent on the costumes,' said Mr Patel. 'You cannae hae kings and the like dressed in any auld things.'

Hamish gloomily paid up. The visit to London had made a hole in his dwindling bank balance. He bought groceries and then decided to take the presents for his mother over to Rogart and spend the day there.

He did not return until the early evening, feeling relaxed and comfortable and full of good food. He wondered how Priscilla would cope with being Lady Macbeth. It was quite a big part to learn.

Waves were mounting on the sea loch and the wind screamed and roared through the blackness of the long northern night.

* * *

The following morning, he took out the present he had bought for Priscilla and went up to the Tommel Castle Hotel.

He found Priscilla in her room, walking up and down, rehearsing her script. She broke off when she saw him.

'You're supposed to knock, Hamish.'

'You never knock at the station. I've a present for you.' He handed her the wood carving.

'This is beautiful. Where did you get it?'

'Up in Grianach. You should take a run up there and buy some stuff for the hotel gift shop. They have grand tweeds as well.'

'I might go over tomorrow. Care to come with me?'

'Fine. I'm not welcome there and was told not to come back, but if you buy stuff, they won't mind seeing me again. How's the play going?'

'I wish I'd never started. I keep reminding myself it's not the Royal Shakespeare Company.'

'You'll be fine. Thon Irishman has left?'

'Yes.' A slight look of guilt appeared in Priscilla's blue eyes. She felt she had led Patrick on only to show one highland constable who had jilted her that she was attractive to other men. She had found it quite difficult to persuade Patrick to leave.

'Are you sure you want to go tomorrow?' asked Hamish. 'Surely you'll be rehearsing like mad.'

'I'll be glad to get away from here for a bit.'

'Why?'

'Why, why, why. Always the copper. If I work hard on the script today and put it all out of my mind tomorrow, then I'll do better than if I worried and worried. Come at nine. I'll get us a picnic lunch.'

The following morning, before Hamish arrived, Priscilla was just finishing her breakfast when she was joined by Harold Jury. 'We've got a hard day's work ahead of us,' he said. 'I'll drive you down to the village hall for the final rehearsal.'

'I won't be there,' said Priscilla. 'I'm going off for a picnic with Hamish and I'm going to put the whole thing out of my mind until this evening.'

'You can't do that. I am the producer and I am ordering you to be at the hall!'

Priscilla stood up. She wavered. Then Harold put an arm around her waist and said softly. 'I know you fancy me, darling, and that's what's making you nervous. Once this play's over, we'll have fun.'

'I've never encouraged you,' said Priscilla.

'Oh, yes you have. I saw you trying to make me jealous by flirting with that Irishman.'

'Get this straight,' said Priscilla, her eyes like chips of ice. 'I've never fancied you, nor will I ever.'

'You're nothing but a prick tease.'

'And you're nothing but a prick,' said Priscilla. 'Get yourself another Lady Macbeth.'

She headed for the door. He caught her arm and twisted her round, his eyes blazing. 'You can't do this to me!'

Mr Johnson appeared flanked by the chef, Clarry, who was wielding a meat cleaver.

'Miss Halburton-Smythe,' said Mr Johnson, 'I believe Hamish is waiting for you.'

Harold released her, his face flaming with rage.

'What's up?' asked Hamish as he climbed into the passenger seat of Priscilla's car after lifting Sonsie and Lugs into the back.

'I'm not going to be playing Lady Macbeth,' said Priscilla. 'Harold *ordered* me to stay for the rehearsal today.'

'You can see his point,' said Hamish awkwardly. 'Or was there anything else?'

'Yes, he got frisky.'

'Oh, dear. Then who is going to play Lady Macbeth?'

'Angela has been understudying.'

'Poor Angela.'

'Hamish, I have just endured a rather nasty scene. Don't mention that damn play again!'

The day was blustery but fine as Priscilla negotiated the zigzag road down to Grianach.

'It's beautiful, Hamish. That's a good natural harbour. Good protection. The waves out there look enormous.'

Priscilla parked by the harbour. Hamish let the dog and cat out and stood breathing in the clean, salty air. James Fringley came striding forward to meet them.

'I thought I told you never to come here again,' he said.

'This is Miss Priscilla Halburton-Smythe,' said Hamish. 'Priscilla, Mr James Fringley, who handles the sales of the stuff. Priscilla here is anxious to give you an order for goods for her hotel gift shop.'

James smiled. 'If you just walk up to the house with me, Miss Halburton-Smythe, I can show you a range of goods.'

'You wait here, Hamish,' said Priscilla.

Hamish sat down on a bollard and looked out over the glittering water. The light's too bright and sharp, he thought. A big storm is coming. While he sat there, a few of the locals appeared, saw him, and sheered away.

Pity, he thought. I could get to love this place almost as much as Lochdubh. How far away it is from the cities, the drugs, and the crime.

He turned last evening's dinner with Anna over in his mind. There was something about the woman that repelled him. It was as if some inner kernel of her was as cold as ice. He had met Russians before, all sorts of warm, jolly people. Still, to have risen to the rank of Inspector must mean she had to be very tough indeed.

Hamish suddenly wanted a cigarette. He wanted to sit smoking and staring out to sea. But he had given up some time ago. I would be stupid to start again. Just the one, he thought. He rose and went into the village shop and said to the troll behind the counter, 'Ten Bensons, please.'

A flood of angry Gaelic erupted from the man, which Hamish translated to mean that if he didn't get out of the shop he would be hit on the head with an axe.

He retreated to the harbour. The craving had gone and he gave a sigh of relief. To think he had nearly blown it.

Priscilla came back with a delighted James Fringley. 'Business is over, Hamish. I think we should go up into the hills for our picnic.'

As she drove off, Hamish asked, 'Where's the goods?'

'He's bringing it over tomorrow. That stuff will sell like hotcakes. I'm even going to put an ad in the *Highland Times*. Christmas is coming, and people will be looking for presents.'

They picnicked on a flat rock in a hollow protected from the wind high up on the moors.

Hamish, watching Priscilla as she efficiently laid out the picnic, thought that she was, for him, rather like cigarettes. Just when he thought the craving had gone, back it would come. He longed to take her in his arms but dreaded rejection. He forced himself to chat lightly about this and that until the yearning went away.

When they arrived back at the hotel, Hamish asked, 'Will you be watching the performance?'

'No, I'm going off to London. I'll tell Mr Johnson about Fringley bringing the stuff for the gift shop.'

'You seem to be able to come and go with that job of yours.'

'I take contracts, Hamish. That's the blessing about being a computer programmer. I'll start another contract when I get back.'

Hamish was torn between relief and sadness that she was going. Without Priscilla around, he could really concentrate on the case.

He decided to call on Angela and see if she was ready for her big part. He found her in her kitchen, sitting in front of her computer as usual.

'What's this?' asked Hamish. 'I thought you would be walking up and down, feverishly remembering your lines.'

233

'I'm not going, Hamish.'

'Why?'

Angela sighed and pushed a lock of hair away from her thin face. 'I just don't want to do it. It's Harold. Why should I bother to help him out when he was so rude to me?'

'How rude?'

'I went up to the hotel yesterday to talk to him about writing. He said to me loftily that he couldn't be bothered wasting the time to talk to me. He said if I was having difficulties, I should wait for inspiration. So when he came tearing down here to tell me to play Lady Macbeth, I told him I hadn't the time because I was waiting for inspiration. I suggested *he* get inspired and find someone else.'

'Unlike you to be so harsh.'

'Hamish, I have met many writers at writers' conventions and not one has blethered on about inspiration. It's hard work, and you just sit down and do it. Every writer knows that.'

Hamish scratched his fiery hair. 'Angela, don't you feel you might be letting the rest of the folk in the village down? They're all so excited about being in a play.'

'Yes, I was struck by guilty conscience, so I phoned him and said if he was absolutely stuck, I would do it. He said harshly he had someone and hung up on me.'

'I wonder who it could be?' marvelled

Hamish. 'No one else has had time to learn the lines.'

'Maybe he's got some actress up from London. Anyway, I'm still mad at him.'

'Writing seems to have stiffened your spine,' said Hamish. 'The old Angela could be bullied into doing anything for anyone. Even your kitchen's still clean!'

'Well, you know how it is. I think I am a real writer at last. I sit down at the computer and am overcome by a burning desire to defrost the fridge.'

'Keep at it. I'll be going to the play tonight. What about you?'

'I can't now, Hamish. What if it's a dreadful failure and everyone blames me for letting them down?'

'I'm sure the ambitious Harold will have found someone.'

Chapter Twelve

*The glass is falling hour by hour, the glass
will fall forever
But if you break the bloody glass you won't
hold up the weather.*

— Louis MacNeice

The wind had roared away earlier and now
mist was creeping up the loch, making the
dark evening even darker. Hamish was glad
they had a calm night for the performance
because he had checked his barometer and the
glass was falling.

He walked along to the church hall. He wondered whether the murderer would try to kill
him again.

People were streaming out of cottages, and
the air was full of excited chatter. I don't like
Harold, thought Hamish, but he's certainly
brought a bit of excitement to the village.

The men had all put on their best suits; some
of the women were even wearing their church

hats. Hamish was in casual clothes and wondered whether he should go back and change but decided against it.

The seating was on a first-come, first-served basis, and he could only get a seat at the back of the hall.

He studied his programme. Priscilla was still listed as playing Lady Macbeth.

The hall was full. He recognized people from other towns and villages in Sutherland. The play had been well advertised in all the local papers.

The school orchestra was murdering the 'Toreador's March' from *Carmen*. Too ambitious, thought Hamish.

At last, they screeched off into silence and the curtains parted. The Currie sisters and Mrs Wellington, barely recognizable in their costumes and make-up as the three witches, began, 'When shall we three meet again/In thunder lightning or in rain? Or in rain?'

'That's our Jessie,' murmured a woman in front of Hamish.

The play proceeded, the lines of Shakespeare sounding odd. Hamish wondered idly whether he had wanted his characters to speak in Scottish accents.

It was amateur, very amateur. Macbeth stumbled over his lines. Matthew, playing Banquo, made a wild gesture and his kilt fell off, revealing a natty pair of boxer shorts decorated with red hearts. The audience cheered. Just when it looked as if the production would degenerate into farce, Lady Macbeth made her entrance.

Hamish sat up straight and peered over the heads of the villagers in front of him. She was tall with long red hair. She began to speak. It was a deep husky voice, mesmerizing, her lines spoken with passion. The effect on the audience was electric.

It was only after half an hour that Hamish realized that Lady Macbeth was not being played by a woman but by Harold Jury himself.

No one bothered about the stumbling actors surrounding Harold. He held the audience from beginning to end, and when he walked forward to take his curtain call and whipped off his wig, there were cries of amazement followed by resounding cheers.

Hamish slid out of the hall and returned to the police station. He needed to think. They had been looking for a woman. What if the murderer had been someone dressed up as a woman?

It couldn't be Harold because he was a well-known author. Surely Harold had been properly checked into. Or had he?

The police, including himself, had not asked where he was on the days of the murders.

239

He decided to go to Strathbane in the morning and consult Jimmy. But Blair would be there, demanding to know what he was doing.

Was Harold one of those multi-talented people? He had acted like a true professional. What size were Harold's feet? Surely not size seven. He was a tall man. He had been wearing a long gown covering his feet.

Hamish hurried back to the hall. He knew there was to be a buffet supper afterwards, the Italian restaurant having generously offered to contribute it.

The actors were still in costume. Harold had his wig on again and was in the middle of an admiring throng.

Willie Lamont was serving out plates of food. He hailed Hamish. 'Wasn't Harold a real Oliver?'

'*Olivier*,' corrected Hamish automatically.

'Have some chicken and penne,' urged Willie.

'Not now,' said Hamish. Willie looked at Hamish in surprise, wondering what was causing him to turn down a free meal.

If only I could see under Harold's dress and get a look at his feet, thought Hamish.

He turned back. 'Any wine, Willie?'

'Aye, look, bottles of the stuff. Help yourself.'

Hamish poured himself a plastic cup of red wine and headed in Harold's direction. Harold saw him approach and smiled, his eyes glittering in his stage make-up.

'Here's our local bobby,' he said.

'I thought you were chust grand,' said Hamish. He stumbled, and his cup of wine shot over the skirt of Harold's costume.

'You clumsy oaf!' yelled Harold.

'Really, Hamish,' complained Mrs Wellington. She took a paper napkin and began to dab at Harold's long velvet skirt.

'It's all right,' said Harold, rapidly recovering from his outburst. 'Red skirt, red wine, no damage done.'

But that skirt still remained over his shoes.

'I'm right sorry,' said Hamish. He pulled his notebook out of his pocket. 'I'd like it fine if you could give me an autograph.'

'Certainly,' said Harold.

Hamish dropped his notebook. He crouched down and stumbled forward, knocking Harold over.

People rushed to help Harold to his feet.

'I'd better go,' babbled Hamish. 'I'm a menace.'

'That you are,' boomed Mrs Wellington.

Hamish fled the hall. His heart was beating hard. When Harold had tumbled over, it was revealed he was wearing a pair of women's shoes with low heels – and Hamish was willing to bet they were size seven. One thing was for sure: Harold had small feet.

He went back to the police station, got into the Land Rover, and headed off through the

241

night to Strathbane. Jimmy lived in a flat near the police headquarters.

Hamish mounted the stairs and rang the bell. Jimmy answered the door, his eyes blood-shot and a strong smell of whisky emanating from him.

'Hamish! What's up?'

'Let me in, Jimmy, and I'll tell you.'

Jimmy listened carefully and then said, 'I'll put some coffee on. I need a clear head.'

He went off to the kitchen and came back with two mugs of black coffee.

'Now, let me get this straight,' he said. 'You see Harold Jury acting as Lady Macbeth. He's got small feet. So you immediately decide that he might be a murderer. He's a fairly well-known author, Hamish.'

'Not that well known. He was only nominated for the Booker.'

'What are you getting at? That he might not be Harold Jury? He was interviewed by Strathbane Television, and no one popped up to say that man is an impostor.'

'Humour me, Jimmy. I daren't go down to London again. Phone the Met in the morning without Blair hearing you and get someone to go round to his flat and check with the neighbours for a description.'

'No need for that. There's probably a photograph of him on the Internet.'

Jimmy switched on the computer. Hamish waited anxiously. 'Here we are. It's Harold all right.'

'Let me see.'

'There he is at the awards ceremony.'

'It's hard to tell from that photo,' said Hamish. 'Looks the same. Hey, look at his feet. Can you enlarge that?'

'Sure.'

'See!' said Hamish, practically quivering with excitement. 'Normal large feet.'

'You mean our Harold may have stolen the real Harold's identity?'

'Could be.'

'Look, Hamish, I'll go to the hotel in the morning and take his fingerprints. If he is who he says he is, we'll look right fools. Also, I'll need a right good excuse to ask for his fingerprints. If he refuses and phones Strathbane, and I have to explain your mad idea, I'll get a rocket for going along with it.'

'I tell you what, I have the fingerprint kit. I'll get the manager to tell me when he's out of his room. I'll lift a print and bring it over to you.'

'Don't get caught, whatever you do. I'm sobering up and the soberer I get, the dafter your idea seems!'

* * *

Hamish barely slept that night. He headed to the hotel first thing in the morning and went into the manager's office, carrying his fingerprint kit in a bag.

'You're up early,' said Mr Johnson.

'I've a favour to ask. I want to get into Harold Jury's room while he's out.'

'He's out all right. He left in the middle of the night. Asked the night porter for his bill and cleared off.'

'Get me to that room before the maids clean it! And give me a description of the car he was driving and the registration number.'

The hotel room was neat and tidy, and the bed had not been slept in. Hamish took out his fingerprint kit and began to dust the surfaces. He swore under his breath. Everything seemed to have been wiped clean.

Where in a hotel room would even a careful villain forget to wipe? He went into the bathroom and carefully dusted the handle of the cistern on the toilet with aluminium powder. 'Bingo,' he muttered. 'One perfect print.'

He carefully peeled it off, rushed out, and headed to Strathbane after calling Jimmy.

A thinner, whiter Blair came lumbering up while Jimmy and Hamish were searching the fingerprint database. 'Whit's up?' he demanded.

Jimmy explained hurriedly. 'Havers,' said Blair. 'Get back to your village, Macbeth.'

'Anything the matter?' Daviot loomed up behind them.

Jimmy explained again while Blair silently fumed over his superior's habit of gliding silently into the detectives' room.

'Got it!' cried Jimmy. 'Look at this!'

Up it came on the screen. Real name, Cyril Edmonds. Charged in 1999 with sending a letter bomb to his ex-fiancée. Served eighteen months.

'We'd better get the Met round to Harold Jury's address to see what happened to him,' said Hamish.

'I set up roadblocks when you phoned, and the trains and airports are being watched,' said Jimmy. 'We sent out a description of his car and the registration number. The very fact that he wiped his fingerprints off everything in the room he could think of damns him.'

'You should have reported to me first,' howled Blair.

'There wasn't time,' said Jimmy. 'You were out.'

'I'll go and search up in the hills,' said Hamish. 'If he's clever, he'll find a place to hide out until he thinks the hunt is dying down.'

All day long Hamish searched and questioned people in the outlying crofts, but the man he now knew as Cyril had disappeared into thin air.

He had left his pets with Angela before he started his search. She was so shocked when she learned the real identity of 'Harold' that she did not protest.

The wind was beginning to rise as he wearily returned to the police station. His barometer had not lied. He knew from experience that a nasty storm was coming. He decided to relax and have a cup of tea before going to pick up Sonsie and Lugs.

He opened the kitchen door, and stiffened.

'Who's there?' he called.

Cyril Edmonds walked into the kitchen from the living room. He was holding a gun.

'You're a bastard,' hissed Cyril. 'I could have got away with it if it hadn't been for you.'

'I think you are the one who is the genuine bastard,' said Hamish. 'Was Margaret Gentle your mother?'

'Worked that out as well, did you?' sneered Cyril. 'Do you know what she did?'

'Why don't you sit down and tell me?' suggested Hamish.

'You mean why don't you sit down and talk while you think of a way to disarm me?'

'I'm genuinely curious. You are one verra clever man.'

Cyril's eyes glittered. 'Yes, I am, amn't I? I planned this revenge for a long time. Do you know what she did, my precious mother? She'd got pregnant by some lowlife that frequented the nightclub where she worked. Abortions were expensive in those days. She worked as long as she could and then stayed with a barmaid from the club down in the East End. The barmaid wanted a baby so as soon as I was born, I was handed over. No adoption papers. The barmaid and her nasty husband who couldn't have children were to bring me up as their own. Well, right after that, the barmaid became pregnant and had twins. I was forgotten after that. He beat me regularly. When I was thirteen, he let his homosexual brother have the care of me and the abuse started. But I got the brother to pay for my education, I got as much as I could out of him, and then I killed him and dumped his body in the Thames.

'I joined an agency and began to get bit parts in films and television. I hadn't any formal training but I was damn good.

'All I ever thought of was getting even with her. I read about her marriage. I stalked her. I wanted some identity to adopt to finally track her down and not be suspected. I'm not homosexual, but there is a type of homosexual that is easily gulled. I picked up Harold Jury in a pub. He begged me to move in with him. He had a nice flat and lots of money. He had a private income from a trust, which allowed him to ponce about as a writer. Ideal. I chose him because we looked a good bit alike.'

'Where did Irena come in?'

'I studied the comings and goings at the castle. When Irena went out one day on her own to shop, I followed her and struck up a conversation. She hated Mrs Gentle, she said. I asked her why she didn't leave, and she confessed to having a stolen passport. Said she was afraid her old Russian protector would send the boys to hunt her down. We spent a lot of time together. She agreed to help me. I said I would, in return, help her get a visa. She was flirting with Mark Gentle and that worried me a bit. Then she phones me one day and says she's going to marry you. I was terrified she would betray me.

'I told her to meet me down in the cellar and we'd have a celebration drink before she went off to be married. She'd given me a key and she'd found out where the back stairs were.

'She came down to the cellar, saying, "Hurry up. I've got to change for my wedding."'

The wind howled and shrieked around the police station.

'I'd got a bottle of sherry and two glasses laid out. She was in such a hurry that she gulped down a glass of sherry without even noticing that I wasn't drinking. I'd drugged the sherry. She turned to leave and collapsed on the floor. I hit her on the head with a hammer. Then I carried the body over and shoved it in that trunk and piled the others on top of it.'

'How did you get Mrs Gentle to meet you?'

'Easy. That bitch liked power. I'd hidden in the castle at that family reunion and I knew all their voices. So I dressed up as a woman and phoned her and put on Mark Gentle's voice, pleading with her and saying I had to see her. She loved that. I said I would meet her on the cliff at the side of the castle.

'So she turns up all dainty and lovely-old-lady, the act she had perfected.'

Hamish glanced quickly at the coffee machine. He had forgotten to switch it off.

'I loved every minute of telling her who I was. She turned to run and I caught her round the neck, strangled her, and hurled her over the cliffs. My God! The joy of sinking my hands at last into her wrinkled neck and see-ing the fear in her eyes. What are you doing?'

'I'm getting a cup of coffee.'

'You're a cool one. Any last words?'

'Why didn't you clear off? Why the play?'

'Because I loved doing it. I love anything to do with the theatre. I felt safe. I liked being an author. I liked having Harold's money to stay at a posh hotel. It's so remote up here, so far from anything I'd ever known. Safety. Respect-ability. I wanted a bit of that. And that bitch Priscilla led me on.'

'So why kill me?'

'Because I could have got away with it. You didn't fool me with that spilled glass of wine or knocking me over. You wanted to see my feet, and the minute I realized that, I knew you were on to me. You could have seen my feet anytime before but it was because I was dressed as a woman. I have small feet for my height. Dancer's feet. Priscilla told me they were looking for a woman with size seven feet. Before I finish you, what was it Irena told you that was so important?'

Hamish half turned, his hand on the coffee pot.

'She told me nothing. I only put that about to try to flush you out. The mileage you must have covered. Up to Grianach, down to London. Why did you put that amateurish bit of wire over the stairs?'

'I thought that with any luck it might work and if it didn't, it would reinforce the idea that a woman was the culprit, maybe one of the family.'

'Why did you kill Mark Gentle?'

'I had to see him. I couldn't risk leaving any loose ends. I had to make sure Irena hadn't confided in him.

'He invited me in when I said I was Harold Jury. He said he'd heard I was staying up in the Highlands when he was there. I asked him if Irena had said anything about me. He began to look suspicious and asked me what was so important about anything that Irena might have said about me. I had to kill him. Well, let's get on with this.'

In one fluid movement, Hamish threw the contents of the scalding hot coffeepot in Cyril's face.

He screamed as Hamish wrested the gun from his hand. But he stumbled to his feet and lashed out and kicked Hamish full in the stomach. As Hamish doubled over, he heard the kitchen door slam, and as he clutched his stomach and headed in pursuit, he heard the roar of a car engine.

Outside in the hell of the shrieking gale, Hamish doubled over again and vomited. Cursing, he finally straightened up, jumped into his Land Rover, and headed in pursuit.

He took the humpbacked bridge out of Lochdubh at such speed that he bumped his head on the roof of the vehicle. Great sheets of rain were obscuring his view. The windscreen wipers were barely coping.

Hamish could not see the shine of any tail-lights ahead. Would he have gone to the hotel?

He talked rapidly into the police radio as he drove. He screeched across the gravel at the hotel forecourt and rushed inside. The night porter swore that no one at all had come in.

Hamish sat down suddenly in a chair in the

reception. He was sure Harold would not take any of the main roads in case of roadblocks.

Then he thought – the castle! Would he hole up there? It was worth a try.

He got back into the Land Rover and hurtled back out into the night.

He was driving fast along a narrow road leading to the castle when a tree crashed down in front of him, blocking the road.

Swearing, he climbed out. Why should the county of Sutherland, usually bereft of trees, choose to throw this one in his path?

He wrestled to try to move it. It was an old ash tree which had seen many years. In the light from his headlamps, he could see the great broken roots and the branches whipping back and forth as if the tree were a live thing in its death throes.

He switched off the lights and the engine and leapt over the tree, setting out on foot. At times he was blown backwards by the sheer force of the gale.

The air was full of shrieking wind, a hellish noise, as if all the devils from hell had been let loose. He reached the entrance to the drive. A small moon raced out from between the ragged black clouds.

The castle was being buffeted by great waves, huge waves, dashing up the side of the cliff and as far as the top of the building. He could dimly make out a light in the tower window and Cyril's car parked in front. Cyril had gone to earth in Irena's old room.

As Hamish struggled forward against the wind, he felt the ground beneath his feet tremble.

Some instinct called to him to stop. Some voice in his head was calling 'Danger!'

But another voice in his head was calling out, too. 'Are you going to let him get away with it?'

He took another step forward.

And then even above the noise of the storm, he heard a great rumbling and threw himself flat on his face, his hands clutching at the tussocky grass.

He raised his head and, by the light of the racing moon, watched in horror as the whole castle began to slide into the sea while the clifftop crumbled under the battering of the waves. For a brief second, he saw Cyril silhouetted against the window, and then he was gone – gone down with the castle into the depths of the raging sea.

Now the waves were dashing up, trying to eat away more of the land.

Hamish got shakily to his feet. The air was full of spray. He headed back the way he had come, propelled this time by the wind at his back.

When he reached the Land Rover, he found that the radio wasn't working, and he could not get a signal on his mobile phone. For the first time, he realized he was soaking wet. He had left the station wearing only a sweater and trousers.

He reversed away from the fallen tree until he could turn around and headed back to Lochdubh.

He reached the shelter of the police station and rushed to phone Jimmy. Jimmy's voice was faint and crackly, but he said he would be at the police station as soon as possible.

Hamish changed into dry clothes. He took down a bottle of whisky from the kitchen cupboard and put it on the table with two glasses. He checked the stove thoroughly before he lit it in case Cyril had left another bomb in there.

Half an hour later, Jimmy came crashing in.

'Two police cars blown over in the hunt,' he said. 'You said something about the bastard having fallen into the sea.'

Hamish told him about the end of the castle. 'He was here before that, trying to kill me.' Hamish went on to outline all that had happened while Jimmy opened the whisky bottle and helped himself.

'I thought Blair would have been here organizing things,' said Hamish.

'We couldn't rouse him. His phone was switched off,' said Jimmy. 'Well, thank God he's gone and truly dead. Save the taxpayer a lot of money. No trial. You'd better write down a full statement, Hamish. Before you called, the Met checked on Harold Jury. He's dead. I wonder where our Cyril got that gun?'

'Do you know,' said Hamish, 'that if Cyril had never become so determined to put on that production of *Macbeth*, we'd never have got him? Or if he hadn't had such small feet, I might never have guessed it was him.'

'It's no use phoning air-sea rescue in this storm. Well, I'd better get the men up there anyway and see what I can do. You stay here, Hamish, and get to work on that report.'

When he had left, Hamish went through to the police office and started typing. It took him two hours to write a carefully detailed report. As he typed, he reflected that Mrs Gentle had made herself look guilty. She had decided not to hire a wedding car because she was regretting the expense and planned to drive Irena in her own car. She stopped the caterers going to the cellar because she thought they might pilfer a few bottles. When he had finished, he sent it off to Strathbane, went through to his bedroom, and fell into bed, fully clothed and down into a dreamless sleep, forgetting for the first time that his pets were not with him.

He woke next morning to the crash of the cat flap. He got out of bed to face the reproachful eyes of two animals. He filled their water bowls and then went to shower, shave, and change into his uniform.

He then loaded his pets into the Land Rover, noticing that the waterfront was covered in pebbles, seaweed, and driftwood, hurtled ashore by the storm. The weather had made another of its mercurial changes. The sun shone down from a clear sky.

Hamish drove up to where the castle had been. Scores of Scene of Crime Operatives were there in their blue coveralls, hovering uselessly on the cliff's edge.

Blair was standing there with Jimmy and Andy MacNab. Jimmy hailed him. Blair turned his back as Hamish walked up.

'You can take a look over the edge,' said Jimmy, 'but the sea's still too rough for anyone to go down there. We'll need to wait until low tide. It'll take ages to find the body between the ruin of the castle and the fact that the whole of the clifftop went down with it. Come to think of it, to get to the pillock's body will probably take more money than if there had been a trial.'

Hamish approached the cliff edge and ducked under the police tape. 'Careful,' shouted a policeman. 'It's still not safe.'

Hamish gingerly approached the edge, lay down on his stomach, and looked over. Below, a mass of stones, earth, and grass was being pounded by the waves.

He eased his way back again and stood up and went to join Jimmy. 'Can't we just leave him there? It's going to be difficult to get to him. There was a bit of a beach at low tide, but I don't know whether that will be still there.'

'We'll see what we can do. Here's our lord and master.'

Daviot strode towards them. 'I read your report, Hamish,' he said. 'That was good work.'

Blair stared at his feet scowling horribly. He hadn't had a drink in what seemed like ages, and the craving was strong. He felt that without Macbeth around, he would be restored to the full dignity of his position. It was humiliating for a detective chief inspector to be outclassed by the village bobby.

Hamish Macbeth was behind all his troubles. Hamish Macbeth was the reason he drank.

There must be a way to get rid of him.

Chapter Thirteen

Inspiring bold John Barleycorn!
What dangers canst thou make us scorn!
Wi' tippenny, we fear nay evil;
Wi' usquebae, we'll face the devil!
— Robert Burns

Three days afterwards, the body of Cyril was found washed ashore in a cove north of the castle. The experts judged he must have thrown himself clear when the castle began to fall into the sea.

'That's saved us a lot of money,' said Jimmy, relaxing in Hamish's kitchen. 'It's nice to get back to normal: drugs, prostitution, and gang fights. What will you be doing?'

'Getting around to repairing the storm damage,' said Hamish. 'There are a few tiles off the roof. The henhouse needs fixing.'

'Have the press gone?'

'Thank goodness, yes, apart from a bloke from one of the Sundays, planning an article on Save Our Coastline. Won't make any difference. They don't care much in Edinburgh or London about what goes on in the very north.'

'Did that girlfriend of yours come back up?'

'If you mean Elspeth, she iss not my girlfriend, and she iss mad at me because I didn't give her the story.'

'She'll come round. She always does. Has Blair been to see you?'

Hamish looked alarmed. 'No. Why?'

'He's been trying to reform me. I thought he might have a go at you. He says drink is the devil's tool. He rants at me, clutching a large Bible. I think he's losing it.'

'He'll get over it. He'll soon be back on the drink again and his old grumpy self.'

'The trouble is, he's even grumpier sober. I'd better get off and leave you to your chores. I just called in to see how you were.'

Hamish worked on the roof, replacing slates that had been blown off in the storm. Then he decided to walk along and visit Angela.

It was one of those white days in the Highlands, veiled behind thick misty cloud. Although the day was quite bright, no sun shone. The waters of the loch had subsided into a glassy calm as if the storm had never existed. The little whitewashed cottages along the waterfront looked as trim as ever, and columns of peat smoke rose from chimneys straight into the white sky.

Two seals floated on their backs in the loch, the idle flapping of their flippers sending out little ripples over the calm. A lot of the old people still believed that the dead came back as seals.

Hamish paused at the stone wall over the beach and watched them. It wouldn't be a bad life, he thought. Just float around and catch fish. He thought maybe he'd take a boat out later and catch some fresh mackerel.

Angela looked pleased to see him and anxious to hear all the details of the death of Cyril. As Hamish talked, it all seemed very far away – the image of the castle tumbling into the sea like something remembered from a film at the cinema.

When he had finished talking, Angela said, 'Poor Harold Jury. The sales of his last book have rocketed. Maybe that's the writer's recipe for success. Die violently. Did the press bother you much?'

'No. They were mostly up taking pictures of where the castle went over and going to press conferences in Strathbane.'

'I saw one of those conferences on television. Blair was talking to them and taking all the credit.'

'He aye does that.'

'Doesn't it make you mad?'

'Not really. The powers-that-be always begin to believe Blair solved any case that I might have had a hand in. It's better that way. Too much exposure and they really would drag me off to Strathbane. It's hard to believe that things are back to normal. It seems as if I've been frightened for quite a long time.'

'You never go on like a frightened man.'

'Oh, it's the grand thing to be frightened. Keeps one's wits sharp.'

Blair was thinking about Hamish Macbeth and wondering how to get rid of him. Murder was out of the question. There must be some way he could get him pounding the beat in Strathbane, just an ordinary copper. Then he thought, if Hamish went missing, after a decent period they might sell that station of his. But how to work it so that no suspicion fell on himself was difficult.

He was leaving police headquarters with Jimmy to investigate a warehouse down at the docks where a tip-off had told him there were drugs stored, when a prostitute called Ruby McFee was being marched into the station by WPC Aileen Drummond.

Blair knew Ruby of old. She was in her forties and suffering from the wear and tear of pounding the streets in all weathers looking for punters. She was a blowsy woman with a round red face and thick blonde hair showing black roots. Her eyes were small and bloodshot.

'Caught again, Ruby,' said Blair.

'Bugger off,' she said.

Blair shrugged and went on out of headquarters.

The tip-off turned out to be rubbish, and the rest of the day was spent in various routine enquiries. Blair finally settled in his flat in front of the television set that evening with a cup of tea. But there was nothing on the box he wanted to see. He switched it off and turned his mind to the problem of Hamish Macbeth.

God to Blair was a sort of senior detective who sat somewhere up there, looking remarkably like Blair himself. He put one hand on his Bible and prayed for a solution to his problem.

All at once, a splendid idea entered his mind.

Ruby emerged from the sheriff's court in the morning to find Blair waiting for her.

'Whit now?' she demanded truculently.

'I've a proposition for you,' said Blair.

'I don't give free blow jobs any mair.'

'It's not that. Get in the car.'

He drove her rapidly out of town and up into the moors. Then he stopped the car. 'There's a lot of money in this for you, Ruby, and no hard work.'

'So what is it?'

'I'll tell you.'

Hamish returned to the police station that evening after having treated himself to a meal at the Italian restaurant. His phone rang.

A woman's voice said, 'I've had a burglary. I'm at Rhian Cottage on Sheep Road, the other side of Cnothan. I'm that distressed. Come quickly.'

'What is your name?' asked Hamish.

'Just come!' she screamed and hung up on him.

Hamish sighed. Surely it could wait until the morning. He glanced at the clock. It was still only nine in the evening.

He decided to get it over with. Leaving his cat and dog, he set out on the road towards Cnothan. The earlier cloud had cleared, and frost was glittering on the heather at either side of the road.

He drove through Cnothan, remembering that Sheep Road was really just an unsurfaced track. He knew there was no sign on the road, and he couldn't remember anyone living there. When Cnothan had been added to his beat, he had memorized every road in the neighbourhood.

He bumped along the track. His headlights picked out a dilapidated cottage at the very end. Anything stolen from a dump like that, thought Hamish, can't really be worth stealing.

As he switched off the engine and climbed out, a woman came out to meet him. She was wearing an old-fashioned pinafore and had her hair covered in a headscarf that shadowed her face.

'I'm glad you've come.'

Hamish walked towards her. 'When did this happen?'

'I was ower in Strathbane and just got back. Come in and see what the bastards have done. They've trashed the place.'

She held open the door. Hamish walked in. He found himself in a room, empty except for a table and two chairs. 'What ...?' he was beginning to say when a savage blow struck him on the back of the head and his world went black.

Angela Brodie opened the door the next morning. Lugs and Sonsie stared up at her.

'This is too much,' complained Angela. 'Come along. I'm taking both of you home.'

She marched along to the police station and knocked on the door. There was no answer.

She felt for the key in the gutter and opened the door. 'In you both go,' she ordered.

But the animals stood there, staring up at her. Perhaps Hamish was still asleep. Angela walked into the bedroom. The bed had not been slept in. Then she remembered she had not seen the police car.

She returned to Hamish's pets and tried to drag Lugs inside by his collar, but the wild cat hissed furiously, the fur on her back standing up.

Angela backed off. She walked back home. Both of them followed her. She dived into her cottage and shut the door on them.

An hour later, she opened the door. They were still there, and it was beginning to rain. 'Oh, come in,' she said. 'But don't you dare frighten my cats!'

Throughout the day, Angela kept returning to the police station. At last she phoned Strathbane but was told that as far as they knew Hamish had not gone out on any job.

She kept the dog and cat for the night and tried again in the morning. To her relief, she saw Hamish's Land Rover parked at the side. Once more she knocked and got no reply. Once more she went in and found the station empty.

Angela went into the police office, found Jimmy Anderson's mobile phone number, and called him.

'Probably poaching,' said Jimmy, 'but I'll drop over later.'

Hamish recovered consciousness. He found he was lying staring up at a dirty ceiling. He cautiously raised his head and then fell back with a groan. He slowly turned his head to find out where he was.

It was a bare room with a bucket in one corner. From the size of the room, he gathered that it had probably been the 'best' room in some croft house. A dining hatch was against one wall, perhaps installed there in the house's better days.

He felt his head. There was a large lump on top of it but the skin did not seem to be broken. He squinted at the luminous dial of his watch. He estimated he had only been unconscious for ten minutes or so, but that had been enough time to drag him in here.

He was wearing only his underwear. Someone had moved quickly. And what was the reason for it?

For the next few hours he rested, occasionally trying to get up and at last feeling strong enough to make the effort. As soon as he could stand, he stumbled across to the bucket and was violently sick. Then he relieved himself and went slowly back to the bed and lay down.

He heard bolts being drawn back, and then, pretending to be asleep and looking under his eyelashes, he saw a tray being pushed through the hatch. The hatch went down. He heard bolts being rammed back into place.

Hamish got slowly up again and went over and examined the tray. It contained a pot of tea, milk and sugar, and two large ham sandwiches.

He gratefully drank the tea but still felt too nauseated to eat anything. He examined the room's tiny window, looking for a way to escape, but it was sealed shut.

He still felt dizzy and sick. He decided to sleep the night and see what he could do about escaping in the morning.

Hamish awoke at seven in the morning. He heard a car arriving, a car door slam, and then the front door of the cottage being unlocked.

Sounds of plates and pans in the kitchen and the sounds of cooking. He put his plate with the uneaten sandwiches on the ledge in front of the hatch. If his captor planned to give him breakfast, then he could grab whoever it was through the hatch. But he didn't know how many people were responsible for his kidnapping. Better to wait and see if they or he or she left the cottage and then try to escape.

Again the double doors of the hatch opened.

He could see a head covered in a black bala-clava. His old tray disappeared, and another was pushed through.

He found he was hungry. There were two bacon baps and a pot of tea. He ate and drank and waited.

The room was cold, so he wrapped himself in the filthy blankets from the bed.

He waited and waited while the late winter sun rose and shone in through the window. Then he heard the front door slam and a little after, the sound of a car driving off.

He walked over and examined the double doors of the hatch. He needed something to force those doors and break the bolts.

Hamish looked down at the tray. It was made of heavy metal, the kind used in hotels and restaurants.

He carefully removed everything off it. He went over to the hatch and rammed the tray at the doors. They gave slightly. He went on using the heavy tray as a battering ram, time after time, pausing only to rest because he still felt weak.

Finally, frightened and furious, he struck at the hatch doors with all his might. They crashed open.

Panting, he waited a moment. Then, glad he was slim, he heaved himself through the open space and tumbled on to the floor on the other side.

It was the same bare room he had seen when he had arrived, but it had been augmented by a camping stove and a small television set.

The front door was, of course, locked. He wondered if the woman had been working alone and if she had put his clothes anywhere. He went into a small bedroom. There was an old wardrobe and an unmade bed. He opened the wardrobe and saw his uniform and boots lying at the bottom. He hurriedly dressed, listening all the while for the car returning. His belt with his police radio and all his other equipment was there. He strapped it on. In his pocket, he found his mobile phone and called Jimmy.

Quickly, he told Jimmy where he was.

'Found Macbeth!' Jimmy shouted to the detectives' room. 'Come on, Andy, and get a couple of coppers. We'd better get to him fast.'

Blair sat as if turned to stone. Then he suddenly seemed to recover from his shock. He rushed outside to the car park, got into his car, and phoned Ruby.

'You let the bastard get away,' howled Blair. 'Don't go back there. Did you use gloves?'

'The whole time,' wailed Ruby. 'What'll I do?'

'Just go home. I'll call on you later.'

Hamish heard the welcome sound of sirens. Then he heard the battering ram striking the front door; after a few blows, it crashed open.

'Are you all right?' asked Jimmy.

'I was knocked unconscious. I'm a wee bit shaky.'

'We'll take you to the hospital. I'll get this place dusted for prints. Any idea who the hell is behind this?'

'Not a clue,' said Hamish. 'It was a woman who answered the door to me. I couldn't get a good look at her.'

'Don't worry. We'll find her.'

'I think you should get the other police cars away somewhere and come back on foot,' said Hamish. 'If we wait here, we'll catch her – or them.'

The owner of the cottage was tracked down. He said a woman had paid him cash for a three-month rent and had left a month's deposit. He had rented it cheap because the place was in such a mess; he'd planned to get the house demolished and then sell the ground as a building plot.

Asked where the contract was, he said the woman had told him they needn't bother, and he was too glad of the money to insist.

Blair sweated it out, terrified all the time that the search would lead to Ruby. They had footprints but no fingerprints, and footprints weren't on file.

He wasn't too nervous about them finding any DNA, because the forensic lab was one of the most inefficient in Scotland. They were backed up with requests for DNA anyway, and most of the results were taking over a year to arrive.

Hamish and Jimmy waited all that day and far into the night, but no one came. 'Maybe whoever it is passed the police cars on the road and decided not to go back,' said Jimmy.

He drove Hamish back to the hospital in Strathbane. Hamish was examined and given painkillers. 'We'll need to take that Land Rover of yours away and give it to forensic,' said Jimmy as they left the hospital.

'What'll I do for transport?'

'I'll try to get someone over with an unmarked police car. Who on earth do you think was behind this? Someone associated with Cyril?'

'No, if it had been someone associated with Cyril, I feel I might be dead now. It was all very amateur. I feel in my bones that the woman was the only one in the cottage.'

Blair was beginning to feel very uneasy. Daviot was raging about a police officer being kidnapped. The forensic team had been sent back to the cottage to go over it again.

In the evening, he made his way to Ruby's flat by a circuitous route. 'This is a mess!' shrieked Ruby. 'It was on the telly. If they get me, they'll lock me up and throw away the key. If they get me I'll have tae say it was you.'

'It won't come to that,' said Blair soothingly. 'I want you to write something and then it'll be all over.'

Daviot called Blair into his office the following day. 'There's been a development,' he said. 'This letter, addressed to me, was handed in by a small boy. He said a woman gave him a pound to deliver it. Unfortunately his description of her could apply to every woman in Strathbane.'

Blair read the letter out loud, just as if he did not already know every word of it.

'Dear policemen,' he read. 'I'm sorry about Macbeth but he led me to believe he would marry me and then he cheated on me. I won't do nothing like that again. A Friend.'

'Dearie me,' said Blair. 'Our Hamish has been at it again. He's a devil with the women.'

'I did hear something to that effect.' The one time Hamish had ridden high in the super-intendent's esteem was when he had been engaged to Priscilla Halburton-Smythe, for

Daviot was a snob. He was furious and amazed when Hamish broke off the engagement. Then there was this unsavoury business of Macbeth trying to marry a hooker.

'I think we should keep this quiet,' said Daviot. 'If it got out, it would be a slur on the whole force. Also, the gangs are joining up with the neo-Nazis to attack immigrants. That should be our first priority. Tell Anderson and the others that we can no longer spare any time on Hamish's kidnap.'

'We've put a policeman on guard outside Macbeth's station.'

'Call him off now!'

Hamish was about to take a cup of tea out to PC Logan on guard outside when the man met him at the kitchen door.

'I've been called off,' he said. 'They're standing down the investigations.'

'Why?'

'Trouble with the gangs.'

After he had gone, Hamish sat down to think. But he could feel a migraine coming on, a result of the blow to his head. He quickly swallowed two migraine pills and went to lie down in his darkened bedroom.

He fell asleep at last and woke later, feeling better. His dog and cat now followed him everywhere. He turned his mind again to the problem as to why the investigation into his kidnapping had been abruptly ended. He left a message on Jimmy's mobile phone, begging for information.

Jimmy phoned back an hour later. 'I don't know what happened, Hamish. One minute it was all systems go on your case, and the next we were being told to stand down. Blair knows something. All I could find out was that a letter to Daviot was delivered this morning. Blair was summoned, and after that everything to do with you stopped. I've looked for that letter but there's not a sign of it, and no report has been written.'

'Whoever it was didn't seem to want to kill me, just keep me prisoner,' said Hamish. 'What would have happened if I'd been kept there several months, say?'

'If you'd ever got out of it, you'd have probably found they'd have closed up your station.'

'Blair!' said Hamish suddenly. 'I bet he's behind this.'

'Come on, Hamish. That's going a bit too far.'

'Does Blair know any woman, sort of thickset?'

'Women run at the sight of Blair. The only people he knows are the prostitutes he used to nick when he was on the beat.'

'Like who?'

'I was leaving headquarters with him and he stopped to speak to one being brought in by Aileen Drummond.'

'Do me a favour and get her name and address.'

Hamish drove down to Ruby's flat in the docks. It was raining hard. He climbed up the stairs, wrinkling his nose at the smell. He hoped she had decided not to go out on her beat in such a filthy night. Maybe she didn't have to. If Blair was behind this, he thought, then he would have had had to pay her and pay her well.

He knocked on her door. A cautious voice from the other side asked, 'Who is it?'

'Blair,' said Hamish.

The door swung open. Ruby let out a gasp as she recognized Hamish and tried to shut the door but he jammed his foot in it, wrenched it open, and forced her back into the room.

Ruby went and sat down on a sofa. She lit a cigarette with trembling fingers while Hamish locked the door and came to stand over her.

'How did you ken?' she asked.

Hamish pulled up a chair and sat opposite her. 'Why did you let Blair put you up to this?' he asked.

'He asked me tae do it,' said Ruby. 'You cannae refuse a polis.'

She crushed out the cigarette and began to cry. Hamish watched her heaving figure unsympathetically. He did not believe in tarts with hearts, and his recent experience with Irena had really soured him.

'I don't want to go to p-prison,' wailed Ruby.

Hamish saw a box of paper tissues on the sideboard and took it over to her. 'Pull yourself together,' he said.

Ruby gulped, shuddered, blew her nose, and wiped her eyes. 'Can I have a wee dram afore you take me in?'

Hamish went back to the sideboard where there was a row of bottles. Blair must have been generous, he thought cynically, because Ruby can't be making much on the streets these days.

Ruby asked for a rum and Coke. Hamish poured her a reasonable measure and took it back to her.

She gulped it down. He saw the fear in her eyes and felt a reluctant twinge of pity.

'How did you get into the life, Ruby?'

'I wisnae always like this,' said Ruby. 'Ruby McFee is no' my real name. I was born Mary Ashford and I was a nice child. This was down in Glesca. My dad died and my mother married again. When I was fourteen my stepdad took me round to his brother, Shuggie Leith, saying I had to stay with him for a bit. The brother raped me, his pals raped me, and then they put me on the streets. One o' my punters fell for me, a nice wee man called Sandy McFee who worked on the Clyde ferries. I ran away with him and we lived in a wee flat in Gourock. We werenae married but I took his name. He called me his ruby and so I became known as Ruby McFee.

'I came back from the shopping one day and he was lying at the foot o' the stairs leading up to our flat wi' his throat cut. I didnae call the polis. I was that frightened. I thought they'd think it was me what done it and find out about the hooking.

'I packed up my stuff and came up here. I don't know if Shuggie and his pals killed Sandy but I never wanted him to find me. Somehow I just drifted back into the life again.'

Hamish sat staring at her. Here was his perfect opportunity to get his revenge on Blair. Blair as well as Ruby would go to prison. But Daviot, he knew, would blame him for bringing the force into disgrace. Somehow, Hamish would share that disgrace, and a vengeful Daviot might move him to Strathbane.

Ruby eyed him nervously, finished her drink, and mutely held out her glass for more. Hamish went to the sideboard and refilled it, his brain racing.

He handed her the glass and sat down and looked at her. 'How would you like to be a respectable married woman?' he asked.

'Stop making fun o' me.'

'I'm serious.'

'That was always a dream I had when I was out in the streets, particularly in the winter.'

'Does Blair know your real name?'

'No. Why?'

'Were you ever charged under your real name?'

'No. When I was hooking in Glesca I was that young, somehow the polis never picked me up.'

'Here's what I want you to do. I want you to write and sign a confession. Then I want you to go out tomorrow and get yourself some lady-like clothes and dye your hair a respectable brown. Then I want you to phone Blair and tell him he's got to marry you or you'll tell all. Don't mention my name. I'll keep your confession as security. You'll tell him that you've written a confession and you've lodged it with a lawyer with instructions it's to go straight to the police if anything should happen to you. Tell him about your real name and that no one will associate you with Ruby McFee.'

'He'll kill me!'

'He can't. He wouldn't dare. You'll never have to walk the streets again.'

Epilogue

*A man cannot be too careful in the
choice of his enemies.*
– Oscar Wilde

Christmas was over, the New Year's celebrations were over, and a fine drizzle of snow was falling: tiny little flakes that spiralled upwards in the freezing air.

Hamish was coming back down to the station from the field at the back after giving his sheep their winter feed when he saw Jimmy standing on the doorstep.

'Let me in out o' this cold, Hamish,' said Jimmy. 'You'll never believe what I have to tell you!'

They walked into the kitchen. Hamish took down the bottle of whisky and warned, 'One dram only, Jimmy. The roads are bad. You could've phoned.'

'Not wi' news like this. Brace yourself,

Bridget, as the Irishman said to his missus by way of foreplay.'

They sat down at the table. Jimmy took a sip of whisky and said, 'Blair's getting married!'

'Michty me!' exclaimed Hamish, affecting surprise. 'Who to?'

'Decent enough body called Mary Ashford. Bit of an eccentric, mind you. I knew she was going to be at the Rotary Club dinner so I wangled an invitation from my pal and took Aileen Drummond along – you know, the PC you promised to take to dinner and never did? Anyway, there's the happy couple on either side of Daviot. Well, the first course was artichoke and Mary begins to eat the whole thing. Then she cries, "Bugger this stuff. It's like trying to eat holly!" Mrs Daviot on the other side of Blair looks shocked. She says, "You're not supposed to eat the whole thing, Mary. Just the bottoms of the leaves." Blair rounds on her and hisses, "Stop showing me up." Mrs Daviot springs to Mary's defence. "Really," she says, "Mary's not the only one who doesn't know how to eat it." And sure enough, some of Strathbane's finest are trying to chomp down the whole thing as well.

'"There you are, darlin'," says Mary, blowing Blair a kiss, and he looks as if he could murder her.'

'Where did he meet her?' asked Hamish, relishing every moment of the account.

'She was working in one of the super-markets and even doing voluntary work in one of the charity shops at the weekend. Mrs Daviot was most impressed. She's organizing the wedding for them.'

'And when is it to be?'

'February the second at St Andrew's kirk in Strathbane. Blair wanted a registry office wedding but Mrs Daviot wouldn't hear of it.'

'Any chance of an invite?'

'I'll see if I can wangle one for you. Now I'm off before the snow gets worse.'

Hamish received an invitation to the wedding. Along with the invitation came details of the wedding present list and the website details of a shop in Strathbane. He got on to the site and ordered a soup tureen out of a dinner service list, putting in his credit card details and instructions for it to be sent off with the message, 'Oh, Happy Day, from your friend and colleague, Hamish Macbeth.'

At last the great day arrived. Hamish put on his only suit and travelled to Strathbane.

It was a day full of blustery wind and yellow glaring sunlight. The church was full. Hamish chatted to people he knew and then found himself accosted by Aileen Drummond. 'What about dinner?' she asked.

'All right. Come over to the station tomorrow evening at seven o'clock. Do you want me to pick you up?'

'No, I'll drive over.' She gave him a saucy look. 'If I drink too much I can stay the night.'

And why not? thought Hamish as he settled into a pew. The hell with romanticism. What I need is some healthy sex.

The organ in the loft struck up, and Hamish twisted his head to get a look at the bride. Mary – he must forget that she was once Ruby – came sailing up the aisle in all the splendour of a white wedding dress and veil. Daviot was to give her away. Mrs Daviot was maid of honour, and Jimmy was best man.

Blair, as he turned to watch his bride approach, looked white and strained.

The service was long. The address to the couple by the minister seemed to go on forever. The hymns were of the dirge variety.

Then it was over. The couple went into the vestry to sign the register.

The organ struck up Mendelssohn's 'Wedding March' and down the aisle came a triumphant Mary. She had lost weight, and her face shone with happiness.

I've done a good thing for once in my life, thought Hamish. And after her experience on the streets, she should be able to handle Blair.

As Blair walked past Hamish, he looked at him, his eyes glittering with suspicion.

The reception at a hotel in Strathbane was a merry affair. The cake was cut, speeches were made, dinner was served, and then the dancing began, Blair and Mary taking the floor. Blair felt he had been sober for a hundred years. The Blair-God up in the sky who had sustained his sobriety was fading fast.

He had asked Mary time after time if Hamish Macbeth ever knew who was behind his kidnapping, but each time she had vehemently replied that he knew nothing.

He returned to his table after the dance. A large fresh bottle of mineral water was sitting beside his plate. He rose and went over to the bar. A bottle of malt whisky glittered in the lights. What was it the highlanders called it? *Usquebaugh* – the water of life. That was it.

'May I help you?' asked the barman.

'I'll help myself,' said Blair. He opened the bottle, filled up a glass, and took a great swallow, feeling the blessed liquor course through his body right down to his toes.

People said later they had never seen Blair in such fine form. He danced the Eightsome Reel, the Gay Gordons, and the Dashing White Sergeant as if his feet had wings.

When he finally retired to the honeymoon

suite in the hotel with his bride, Blair stumbled across to the bed, fell across it, and lay there snoring. Mary carefully hung away her wedding dress, had a bath, and put on not the honeymoon nightgown, but a serviceable flannelette one.

She undressed her snoring husband down to his underwear. With a contented little smile, she took her knitting out of her suitcase, turned on the television, and proceeded to knit.

Marriage was good.

The following evening, Aileen arrived exactly at seven o'clock. Unfortunately, Aileen was one of those women who look more attractive in uniform than out of it. When she shrugged off her coat in the restaurant, she showed she was wearing a pink boob tube decorated with sequins. Her navel was decorated with a fake ruby, very much in prominence as a roll of fat bulged over her tight Lycra trousers when she sat down. She had put pink streaks in her hair, and her eyelashes were so heavily mascaraed, it looked as if two large spiders had found a home in her face.

Oh, God, I wish something would happen to get me out of this, prayed Hamish, hiding his face behind a menu.

Willie's face when he took the order was a tight mask of disapproval.

Aileen chipped in and said they'd have a bottle of Valpolicello to start. 'Hear you're quite a lad with the ladies,' she said when Willie had left.

'All lies,' said Hamish. 'I'm quite shy really.'

'Come on, laddie. Shy men don't get engaged to hookers.'

Her voice rang round the restaurant. The other diners listened avidly.

Hamish was just wondering if he could fake illness when to his amazement, Anna Krokovsky walked into the restaurant. He did not like her but in that moment he looked on her as his saviour.

She was out of uniform. 'May I join you?' Ignoring Aileen's scowl, she pulled up a chair and sat down.

'Aileen, do you know Inspector Krokovsky?' asked Hamish.

'I've seen you around,' muttered Aileen.

'I thought you had gone back to Russia,' said Hamish.

'I had, but I am here with a special invitation. You are invited to Moscow. We would like to study your methods.'

'How long for?'

'A few months. Mr Daviot says officers from Strathbane can cover your beat.'

This was worse than the prospect of a night with Aileen, thought Hamish miserably. Blair would work furiously during those months to

287

prove that the station in Lochdubh was not needed.

'It's verra kind of you,' he said awkwardly. 'But I'm afraid I must refuse.'

'Why?'

'I would like to talk to you in private. Maybe afterwards.'

'No, now.' She turned to Aileen. 'Would you mind leaving us?'

'Whit!' screeched Aileen. 'I'm on a date.'

'Do you want me to phone Superintendent Daviot?'

Aileen glared at Hamish, who was studying the tablecloth. Then she threw down her napkin.

'Never, ever speak to me again, Hamish Macbeth.'

Hamish got to his feet to help her on with her coat, but she pushed him away. Under the fascinated eyes of the diners, she rushed to the door and slammed it so hard behind her that the whole room seemed to vibrate.

Anna sat unmoved.

Hamish began to speak, but Willie arrived with the starters. 'I may as well eat what she has ordered,' said Anna. 'Your taste in women is not what I would have expected.'

'Let's get down to this,' said Hamish. 'I cannot go. I am begging you not to press the matter. I have fought and fought until I am weary to keep the police station open here.

288

You like my methods or you would not have got this invitation for me. If I go away for several months, they will find a reason to close the station. I will be put on the beat in Strathbane. There will be no one to deal with this vast area, no one to look after the old people in the outlying crofts. They talk about community policing in Strathbane but they really don't have the first idea how to go about it.

'Did you come all this way just to invite me?'

Anna suddenly smiled. 'Not exactly. Scotland Yard need Moscow's advice on the mysterious death of a Russian in London. You look wretched. Eat your food and we will forget about the matter.'

'But what will Daviot say?'

'I will say I have been called back to London and will approach you about the visit some other time.'

Hamish let out a slow breath of relief.

She began to question him about the death of Cyril and listened carefully while he described how he had discovered that Cyril had stolen Harold Jury's identity.

'Amazing,' she said when he had finished. 'But did you not notice his small feet before?'

'I had no reason to be looking at men's feet,' said Hamish. 'It was seeing him dressed as a woman to play the part of Lady Macbeth that gave me the idea. Also, it was not just that he was good in the part of Lady Macbeth, he almost was Lady Macbeth, if you know what I mean. There was something cold and murderous about him. He was mad, of course. It wasn't just because of his rotten upbringing. Lots of kids have rotten upbringings and go on to be decent citizens. I think he really was a dangerous psychopath. He'd need to have been to go around killing all those people. But he was clever. He played the part of that author so well.'

'But why, when he had finished what he came to do, murder his mother, did he hang around?'

'I think he fell in love – or as much as a character like that could fall in love – with Priscilla Halburton-Smythe.'

'Ah, the blonde beauty.'

'Then he loved acting, and the production of the play got him close to Priscilla and kept him in the limelight, even though it was only the limelight of a small village. Also he hated me for playing a trick on him.' Hamish told her about the 'highland welcome'.

Anna laughed. 'If he was that clever, why did he fall for a stupid prank like that?'

'Because he was acting the part of Harold Jury. God rest his soul, but I think Harold Jury must have been pretty pretentious.'

At the end of the meal, Hamish asked, 'Where are you staying? Can I drive you somewhere?'

'I am staying in Inverness. I have a car and driver waiting.'

Hamish waved her goodbye with relief and started to walk towards the police station. Then he froze. Aileen's car was still parked outside, and the engine was running. She must be inside her car, running the heater, and waiting for me, thought Hamish. No doubt, she really wants to tell me what she thinks of me.

Huddled in his coat, he set off on the long walk up to the Tommel Castle Hotel to beg once more for a room for the night.

The next morning when he walked back to the police station, snow was beginning to fall. Winter was moving back into Sutherland. It looked as if the spring would never come.

Aileen's car was gone. He set about doing his chores. The snow became a blinding blizzard.

It raged all day and then by evening, it roared away to the east. Hamish dug a path outside the police station, leaned on his shovel, and looked along the waterfront. Everything was white and glittering under the moon. He felt the village and landscape had been in some way sanitized by the snow, swept clean of murder and strangers and blood.

With a comfortable feeling of being safe at home at last, he went in and locked the door.

If you enjoyed *Death of a Gentle Lady*, read on
for the first chapter of the next book in the
Hamish Macbeth series . . .

DEATH
of a WITCH

Chapter One

By the pricking of my thumbs,
Something wicked this way comes.
   – William Shakespeare

Police Constable Hamish Macbeth, heading home to his police station in the village of Lochdubh in Sutherland, heaved a sigh of relief. He stopped for a moment by the side of the road and rolled down the car window. He was driving a battered old Rover, manufactured before the days of power steering and electronic windows.

Hamish breathed in all the familiar scents of the Scottish Highlands: peat smoke, wild thyme, pine and salt air blown in on the Atlantic gales from the coast.

Urged by his friend Angela Brodie to go abroad on holiday for once in his life, Hamish had opted for a cheap off-season package trip to the south of Spain.

His hopes of a holiday romance had been

dashed as soon as he arrived. The hotel, ambitiously named The Royal Britannia, catered for British old-age pensioners who wanted to escape the winter back home and the heating bills that came with it. He was in great demand at tea dances, as the other guests were mostly sprightly ladies in their sixties and seventies. When he tried to escape from the hotel food, which was designed for the British palate – chips with everything – and went to some little Spanish restaurant, he would find that several of the ladies had followed him only to become amorous over jugs of sangria. Cursed with innate highland courtesy, he could not find it in him to be rude enough to get rid of them.

But now he was heading home. He had bought the old banger of a car to leave at Inverness airport when he started his journey, not wanting to use the police Land Rover and so incur the wrath of his bosses.

Hamish started off again as the car coughed and spluttered, threatening to collapse at each steep hill like a weary horse.

At last he drove over the humpbacked bridge and into the village of Lochdubh.

He uncoiled his long length from the little car and stood up and stretched. Fingers of rain were blowing down the sea loch, but there was a patch of blue over to the west heralding better weather to come. Although it was

November, the proximity of the Gulf Stream meant there were often mild days.

Then for some reason he could not explain, he began to fell uneasy. It seemed that the very air was full of some vague threat.

He shook himself impatiently, unlocked the police station door, and went in.

There was a note from Angela lying on the kitchen table. It read: 'Hamish, this is the very last time I look after your pets for you. Come and collect them as soon as you can, Angela.'

Hamish owned a mongrel called Lugs and a domesticated wild cat called Sonsie. Angela Brodie was the doctor's wife. He went out again and walked to Angela's cottage. The cat and dog looked at him sullenly as if he were not to be forgiven for having left them.

'About time, too,' said Angela crossly.

'They weren't too much trouble, surely?' said Hamish.

'They kept escaping and going to look for you and I had the gamekeeper, Willie, and several of the others up on the braes to hunt them down and bring them back. Oh, well, sit down and have a coffee and tell me about your trip. Lots of sunshine, pretty girls?'

'I'm glad to be home, and I don't want to talk about it,' said Hamish.

The wild cat put a large paw on Hamish's leg and gave a low hiss. Lugs, a shaggy dog with floppy ears and odd blue eyes, stared up at Hamish accusingly.

Hamish sat down at the cluttered kitchen table where Angela's cats roamed among the unwashed breakfast dishes. Looking at Angela, with her wispy hair and gentle face, Hamish wondered, not for the first time, how a doctor's wife could be so unhygienic.

'I had an offer for your cat while you were away,' said Angela, putting a mug of coffee down in front of him. 'Most insistent, she was. Last offer was a hundred pounds.'

'Who are you talking about?'

'Of course, you don't know. We've got a newcomer. She bought Sandy Ross's cottage.'

'Must have got it for a song,' said Hamish. 'That place has only a corrugated iron roof and an outside toilet. Who is she?'

'Catriona Beldame.'

'What sort of a name is that? Is she foreign?'

'No, she has a bit of a highland accent.'

'And where's she from?'

'Nobody knows. She just arrived. She's ... well, odd.'

'How odd?'

'She gives me the shivers. She's very tall, as tall as you, and she has a queer sort of medieval face, very white, and yellowish brown eyes with heavy white lids. She has a long thin nose and a small mouth. She saw your cat and decided she must have it. There's something else.'

'What else?'

'Some of the local men have been seen visiting her late at night.'

'Dinnae tell me Lochdubh's got its own brothel at last!'

'That's not it. I think she supplies herbal medicines.'

'So why men, why late at night? Why no women?'

'That's the odd thing. No one talks about it. The Currie sisters said something to me about the men visiting her and then they clammed up.'

'Not like that precious pair,' commented Hamish. The Currie sisters were spinster twins and usually a great fund of gossip, some of it at Hamish's expense. 'I'd better go and visit this newcomer.'

'If you can find the time. Detective Chief Inspector Blair has been demanding to know when you're getting back. He said that you're to report to police headquarters in Strathbane as soon as you arrive.'

'Why?'

'It might be because some gang has been robbing all the little local post offices in the north. Lochinver was attacked last week and then Altnabuie. You know how it is. They think we're easy pickings this far north and with only one policeman to cover hundreds and hundreds of square miles.'

* * *

Hamish returned to the station, changed into his uniform, helped his pets into the police Land Rover, and set off over the hills.

As he drove down the long slope that led to Strathbane, he thought the town really was a blot on the beauty of the highland landscape with its decaying docks, crumbling tower blocks, vice and crime.

Steady rain was beginning to fall as he walked up the steps of headquarters and made his way up to the detectives' room.

Detective Sergeant Jimmy Anderson cried, 'Well, if it isn't *señor* back from Spain! Bring me a present?'

'Some duty-free whisky.'

'Got it with you?'

'Back at the station.'

Hamish noticed that Jimmy's usually sharp foxy face was getting blurred round the edges and his blue eyes were watery. The amount the detective drank was at last beginning to show.

'What's all this about burglaries?' asked Hamish.

'Lot of them at wee post offices.'

'What's been done about it?'

'Nothing much. The territory's huge and we never know where they'll hit next. Blair wants to see you.'

The man himself lumbered out of his office. He was a thickset Glaswegian who loathed Hamish.

'There you are, you teuchter,' he snarled. 'Anderson, gie him what we've got on thae burglaries. I want a quick result.'

Blair went back into his office and slammed the door.

'I've printed off all the reports for you,' said Jimmy. 'It's always the same. Three men, masked wi' balaclavas. One wi' a sawn-off shotgun. Nobody's been hurt so far.'

'Any undercover cops been sent out to hide in the post offices?' asked Hamish.

'Aye, for a bit. But the villains always chose the one there wasn't a cop in.'

Hamish pulled out a chair and sat down. 'Now, there's a thing. Could it be possible that some cheil here was giving them information?'

'Aw, come on, Hamish. It's hardly the Great Train Robbery we're talking about.'

'Who's the newest policeman on the force?'

'Policewoman. Wee Alice Donaldson.'

'Where is she right now?'

'Off duty today. Och, Hamish. You just can't think . . . '

'Of anything else,' said Hamish. 'Let me have her address.'

Jimmy applied himself to the computer and then said, 'Here it is. Write it down. Eight Bannoch Brae. That's down near the docks. Not a tower block. There's a row of wee houses just before you get to the tower blocks on the Inverness Road.'

'And what's she like?'

301

'Neat, quiet. Come on, laddie. You've had too much sun.'

'It iss worth a try,' said Hamish angrily, the sudden sibilance of his accent showing he was uneasy. 'I haff nothing else to go on.'

'Suit yourself. Did you get laid?'

But Hamish was already walking away.

When Hamish left headquarters, the wind had risen. Rain slashed into his face as he hurried to the Land Rover.

He found Bannoch Brae and parked outside number 8. 'Won't be long,' he said to his animals. 'Sit there and shut up and I'll buy ye a fish supper on the road home.'

There was a weedy garden in front of a small stone house. Hamish went up to the front door and rang the bell.

The door opened and a girl stood looking up at him. She was not very tall. Two wings of black hair hung on either side of a thin face.

'Alice Donaldson?' asked Hamish.

'Yes, that's me. It's my day off. Am I wanted back on duty?'

'No, I chust wanted to be having a wee word with you.'

'Come in.'

She stood aside to let him past and then closed the door and ushered him into a small front room.

The room seemed rather bleak. It was simply furnished with a three-piece suite and a paraffin heater in front of the empty fireplace.

302

'Sit down,' said Alice. 'Tea?'

'No, thank you. I'm chust back from Spain and I haff been asked to investigate the burglaries of the post offices,' said Hamish, nervously wondering why his imagination had leapt to the conclusion that some member of the force had been tipping off the gang.

'Oh, yes? How can I help? I haven't had anything to do with any of the cases.'

Hamish could not see much of her face because of those wings of hair. Didn't they irritate her?

She was wearing a man's shirt tied at the waist and a pair of worn jeans. His hazel eyes suddenly sharpened.

'What are you staring at?' she demanded.

'That looks like a cigarette burn on your neck,' said Hamish.

Her hand fluttered up to the burn. 'It's nothing. I'm clumsy.'

Hamish looked around the room. He could not see any ashtray; neither could he smell smoke. If she smoked, he thought, then the fabric upholstery would have retained some of the smell.

He was sitting at one end of the sofa and Alice was in an armchair next to him.

Hamish leaned forward suddenly and swept a wing of her hair back from her face. There was a black-and-yellow bruise on her cheek. She jerked her head back, and the other wing of hair flew back. The other side of her face was bruised as well.

'Who did this to ye, lassie?' asked Hamish gently.

'No one!' Her voice was shrill. 'I'm clumsy. This is my day off. You've no right ... '

'They beat you up for information, didn't they?' said Hamish. 'Do you know them, or did they just pick on you?'

She began to cry. Great sobs racked her body. Hamish waited patiently. He felt that if he comforted her, she might take it as a sign of weakness.

He took a handkerchief out of his pocket and handed it to her. It had been given to him by one of his admirers at the Spanish hotel who had even embroidered his initials in one corner.

At last she wiped her eyes and looked at him bleakly. 'I'm finished with the force.'

'Let's hear it,' said Hamish.

In a flat tired voice she told him what had happened. She had been out clubbing in Strathbane and had got picked up by a man, George MacDuff. They had gone out for a bit and then one evening he had come round with two friends, Hugh Sutherland and Andy Burnside. George had said the police were staking out post offices and they wanted her to tell them which ones. She refused. George got nasty. They tied her to a chair and stripped off her blouse and began to burn her with cigar-

304

ettes. She said she was terrified and told them she would find out for them.

'You had their names and descriptions,' said Hamish. 'Why didn't you just report them?'

'George knows where my mother lives in Bonar Bridge. He said if I told anyone, they would kill her.'

'Lassie, the police could have put your mother under protection.'

'With Blair in charge?'

'Oh, well, maybe you have a point. What's the next job?'

'They came round today. I said I wouldn't tell them anything more and they beat me. I still wouldn't tell them but they hurt me so much, I told them that the post offices were no longer under surveillance. George said something like "Leave her." Then as they went out, I heard one of the others say, "Braikie tomorrow'll be our last anyway." I'd better get my coat. You'll be taking me in.'

'Let me think.' Hamish ran his long fingers through his flaming red hair. 'Who's your doctor?'

'Dr Sing.'

'Sympathetic?'

'He seemed like a nice man. I only saw him the once when I had a sprained ankle.'

'Get me his number.'

Supplied with the phone number, Hamish phoned Dr Sing and asked him to call, adding that it was a police matter.

'What are you going to do?' asked Alice.

'Try to get you out of this.'

When Dr Sing arrived, Hamish said, 'Miss Donaldson has been beaten up during some undercover work. We fear this might be because of some informant at headquarters. Until we investigate further, we want you to sign her off for two weeks suffering from injuries incurred after a bad fall down the stairs. You would be helping an investigation considerably if you could do this.'

Dr Sing was a young doctor, recently qualified and anxious to please. He wrote out the certificate and would have examined Alice but Hamish said a police doctor had already had a look. 'But the certificate has to be issued by her own doctor,' said Hamish.

When the doctor had left, Hamish said, 'Get over to your mother in Bonar Bridge and get her off to a wee hotel somewhere until this blows over. Now, if these men are caught and your name comes up, don't say I had anything to do with it or we'll both be out of the force.'

'I don't know how to thank you,' said Alice.

'Just move fast and get out of here,' said Hamish. 'Have you got a car?' She nodded. 'Pack quickly and off you go!'

Hamish stopped on the road back to Lochdubh and bought three fish suppers to feed his pets and himself, wondering all the time how to catch the men who proposed robbing the Braikie Post Office. They were getting bolder, he thought. The others had mainly been sub post offices in general stores, but Braikie was a pedigree one and quite new. No one could understand how Braikie, a remote highland town, should get a new post office when the government was proposing to close so many down.

Twice Hamish had been promoted to sergeant and twice he had been demoted. During the two periods he had held the rank of sergeant, he had policemen working under him. One was Willie Lamont, who had married the daughter of an Italian restaurant owner and left to work in the restaurant. The other, Clarry Graham, was now employed as a chef at the Tommel Castle Hotel. He decided to get them to help him. If he got a squad from Strathbane, they would insist on knowing how he got the information about the proposed robbery. Or Blair might take over and make a mess of it.

Hamish had a sudden image of Blair being blasted to death by a shotgun and he smiled. It was great that some of the things inside his head never got to the outside, he thought.

In the morning, Hamish, flanked by Clarry and Willie, broke the news to the alarmed postmistress, Ellie Macpherson, that he expected the place to be raided. Unfortunately for Hamish, Ellie was the leading light of the local dramatic society and also a sort of female Walter Mitty. He had managed to talk to her just before she opened up in the morning. Ellie, a scrawny woman who jangled with cheap jewellery, drew herself up and said, 'I shall throw myself on the guns!' Her eyes were half closed. Hamish repressed a sigh. He guessed Ellie was already seeing herself on the front page of some newspaper.

'You'll do nothing of the sort,' snapped Hamish. 'You'll lie down behind your counter as soon as they come in. Now, Willie and Clarry here will be in the post office, looking at cards or something. They've got their shot-guns and if anyone asks, they'll say they are going out hunting rabbits up on the braes.'

The day dragged on. Hamish, hidden in the back shop, yawned and fidgeted. Willie and Clarry, tired of reading the rhymes of the greeting cards to each other, yawned as well with boredom.

Just when Hamish was beginning to fear that the robbers planned to attack somewhere else, the door of the post office was thrown open. He heard the customers scream and a man's voice say, 'Hand over the money or you'll get shot.'

Hamish darted out of the back of the shop, holding his own shotgun. He trod on the prone figure of Ellie, who screamed.

Willie was holding his shotgun against the

neck of the one armed man who had dropped his gun to the floor, and Clarry was covering the other two. Hamish leapt over the counter and, taking out three sets of handcuffs, arrested and cautioned the robbers.

Blair was furious when he got the news. 'Whit was that loon daein' playing the lone sheriff?' he said to Chief Superintendent Peter Daviot.

'Now, now,' said Daviot. 'Hamish has got these men and I am not going to quibble about the way he did it.'

Jimmy Anderson waylaid Hamish as he was on his way out of headquarters after typing up a full report.

'So was Alice the informant?' he asked.

'No, nothing to do with it. Chust a lucky guess on my part.'

'She's not in today.'

'Och, the lassie had a bad fall. I called her doctor and he told her to take a couple of weeks off.'

'Aye, right,' said Jimmy cynically.

'Come over to Lochdubh one evening,' said Hamish. 'Don't forget, I've a bottle for you.'

Hamish was just sitting down wearily to an evening meal of Scotch pie and peas when someone knocked at the door.

'Come in,' he shouted. 'The door's open.'

Alice walked in. 'I heard about it on the evening news,' she said. 'Did they say anything about me?'

'No, I'd have heard. They're not going to confess to beating someone up for information. They'll all be sent away for a long time. You can get drunk and run someone over in your car and get a suspended sentence, but if you steal money then the full weight of the courts comes down on your head. Sit down. I hope you've eaten, because this is all I've got.'

'Yes, I did have something earlier. So I can move back home?'

'Certainly. None of that lot will be getting out on bail.'

She sat down with a sigh. 'I'm going to hand in my resignation.'

'Why?'

'I'm just not cut out for the force. It's not really because of the beating. I don't have much courage. I'm going back to university to get a degree and then maybe I'll teach.'

'If that's what you want to do ... '

'But we can see each other sometimes?'

'Maybe. I do haff the girlfriend, you know.'

'Oh, well, I'd better be on my way.'

Hamish saw her out, finished his meal, undressed, showered and went to bed, stretching out with a groan of relief. There were two thumps and the cat and dog got into bed with him.

310

A gale was howling outside, wailing round the building like a banshee. Before he plunged into sleep, Hamish found he was experiencing a stab of superstitious dread. Must be that pie, was his last waking thought.

The morning was glittering with yellow sunlight. Wisps of high cloud raced across a washed-out blue sky, and the waters of the loch were churned up into angry choppy waves.

Hamish put on his uniform of serge trousers, blue shirt, dark blue tie and police sweater with epaulettes. He put his peaked cap on his red hair. He noticed that his trousers were baggy at the knees.

He unlocked the large cat flap, big enough to let the dog in and out as well, and said to his pets, 'You stay here. I've got a visit to make.'

The wind sang in the heather as he made his way on foot to Sandy Ross's old cottage. Who was this Catriona Beldame that even the Currie sisters wouldn't gossip about?

He sensed someone behind him and swung round. The seer, Angus Macdonald, his long grey beard blowing in the wind, was shouting something, but his words were whipped away with the gale.

Hamish waited until Angus caught up with him. 'Dinnae go there, Hamish,' panted the seer.

'Why not,' said Hamish, rocking slightly in the force of the wind and holding on to his peaked cap.

'Because she's a witch, that's why,' said Angus. 'She's brought evil to Lochdubh.'

'Havers,' said Hamish. 'What's she doing? Setting up in competition?'

'I'm warning ye, Hamish. Black days are coming. I see blood.'

'Och, away wi' ye,' said Hamish. 'There's no such thing as witches.'

'On your ain head be it,' said Angus and turned away.

Hamish walked on, hoping that old Angus wasn't beginning to suffer from the onset of Alzheimer's.

The cottage had no garden. The springy heather went right up to the door. It was a low one-storey whitewashed building with a red corrugated iron roof.

As he approached the door, a large black cloud swept across the sun and all at once the wind died.

Again Hamish felt that odd stab of superstitious dread. Then the wind started up again and the cloud moved from the sun.

Hamish raised his hand to the weatherbeaten knocker on the door.

To **order your copies** of other books in the Hamish Macbeth series simply contact The Book Service (TBS) by phone, email or by post. Alternatively visit our website at www.constablerobinson.com.

No. of copies	Title	RRP	Total
	Death of a Gossip	£6.99	
	Death of a Cad	£6.99	
	Death of an Outsider	£6.99	
	Death of a Perfect Wife	£6.99	
	Death of a Hussy	£6.99	
	Death of a Snob	£6.99	
	Death of a Prankster	£6.99	
	Death of a Glutton	£6.99	
	Death of a Travelling Man	£6.99	
	Death of a Charming Man	£6.99	
	Death of a Nag	£6.99	
	Death of a Macho Man	£6.99	
	Death of a Dentist	£6.99	
	Death of a Scriptwriter	£6.99	
	Death of an Addict	£6.99	
	A Highland Christmas	£5.99	
	Death of a Dustman	£6.99	
	Death of a Celebrity	£6.99	
	Death of a Village	£6.99	
	Death of a Poison Pen	£6.99	
	Death of a Bore	£6.99	
	Death of a Dreamer	£6.99	
	Death of a Maid	£6.99	
	Death of a Gentle Lady	£6.99	
	Death of a Witch	£6.99	
	Death of a Valentine	£6.99	
	Death of a Sweep (hardback)	£18.99	
Grand total			£

FREEPOST RLUL-SJGC-SGKJ, Cash Sales Direct Mail Dept., The Book Service, Colchester Road, Frating, Colchester, CO7 7DW. Tel: +44 (0) 1206 255 800.
Fax: +44 (0) 1206 255 930. Email: sales@tbs-ltd.co.uk

UK customers: please allow £1.00 p&p for the first book, plus 50p for the second, and an additional 30p for each book thereafter, up to a maximum charge of £3.00. Overseas customers (incl. Ireland): please allow £2.00 p&p for the first book, plus £1.00 for the second, plus 50p for each additional book.

NAME (block letters): _____

ADDRESS: _____

_____

_____ POSTCODE: _____

I enclose a cheque/PO (payable to 'TBS Direct') for the amount

of £_____

I wish to pay by Switch/Credit Card

Card number: _____

Expiry date: _____ Switch issue number: _____